CHASING REDEMPTION

The Chasing Series: Book Two

RM Hamrick

Cover design by Covers by Christian
Editing by Sticks and Stones Editing

To Alledria Hurt, John Calligan, RS, and JC
for their invaluable feedback and support

CHAPTER ONE
ONE GOAL

Audra swept the stray auburn hairs away from her face and ear as she paused on the half-cleared trail. She had been tracking it for a while, but now she could hear its shuffling. The speed of the walk told her it had no purpose to its wandering, but was lost and unfocused. She could relate, but not today.

Today she had one goal. To find one and save its life.

When Audra was a child she wasn't trying to save their lives; she was running from them in these same Georgia woods. Now zombies - zoms - seemed fewer and farther. Audra wondered if Lysent Corp was collecting them ahead of her to protect their business model. Lysent connected rich families with their wandering loved ones - and received a healthy cash sum in return. Audra had stolen their antidote to cure the zoms. Her group replicated and gave it freely, chiseling away at Lysent's corporate bullshit as they could.

And today they could. Today she had one goal.

She heard its snapping of twigs, the rustling of leaves. The fresh litter dusted the ground of years of pine straw. She could even guess it was male - larger feet, heavier legs dragging. She reverted to breathing through her mouth as soon as she got the first whiff. Male or female smelled the same - putrid. The summer drought hadn't allowed many to be rinsed off in afternoon storms, so the products of any bodily functions stuck to the zombies, wounds festered, and odors lingered on their remaining garments.

Soon she spotted her prize, although he hadn't caught a hint of her. Zoms were first and foremost provoked by sight, and she remained behind him. Would this zom voraciously attack when he discovered her or would he be too weak? The chase hadn't been much of a chase lately. It seemed last winter had weakened them and lessened their enthusiasm as hunters. Like most animals, the longer it had gone without eating, the more likely it wasn't going to eat.

Tired of following, she took a chance and let out a sharp whistle. Audra watched him stop before pivoting. She whistled again as he finished his one hundred and eighty degree turn with a wretched stagger and his gray, hollowed face came into view. She waved her hand in a joke greeting. The hair - no, the scalp - had fallen off to the side, revealing a thin layer of dermis over the skull. Otherwise he was intact, skin upon frail bones - disgusting, but salvageable. Clothes hung off his body, gray and indiscernible from his pallor. His rail-thin arms bore deep scratches where he had gotten caught on branches and pulled hard. Audra avoided looking at his eyes with her green ones. They were all the same - dark gray - the same as Belinda's. Audra had already spent days staring into them, trying to find someone, any part of someone, inside.

He shuffled to her, but Audra would not call it a run. Starvation had taken its toll. Audra reached into her bag. In the past, she would have pulled out her biometric reader to determine whether Lysent was interested in the person. Now, it did not matter. Inquired, deposit paid, no family matches available, other people and their actions no longer gave value to your life. The fact that you were here gave you value. You were worth waking up. Audra made sure of it. She retrieved a thick band of cloth to use as rope.

She wouldn't need to pull some clever evasive maneuver at top running speed to take him down. She merely sidestepped his clumsy launch and let him fall. From there she grabbed one wrist and turned him on his back before grabbing the other, avoiding his long, jagged nails. His neck and upper body craned to bite at her. She restrained him with a boot to his chest, gently as not to remove skin from his sternum. She wrapped up his wrists, finishing with a surgeon's knot. He struggled for a moment, like a dying upturned cockroach. How the world must seem different from down there.

The zoms were in pain. That much she and her team knew. Their first non-regulated awakening, Gordon had told them it was as if he had caught fire. Relief was unknown. As they woke up others, they heard similar stories. Did these zoms wander and search for food to ease their constant suffering? The virus tore away will, everything but their most basic desires - to be without pain, to have food, to spread. Audra cocked her head and wondered if she and the zoms were so different. The same virus had torn her from her family. She constantly searched for relief, food, and shelter. They had both lost to the virus. One had just turned gray. Audra wondered if she too would fade away, like this dying specter in the woods. Audra stopped, closed her eyes, and reminded herself who was to blame.

Lysent.

Lysent had created this virus. For what reason, she still did not understand, but she would make sure that it ultimately hurt them in the same way. They would be torn apart, searching for relief, food, and shelter. And then they would fade away into the grayness until it was just a dim spot in their history.

Audra stepped off the zom and twisted him up to kneeling before helping him to his feet. She was caught off guard and off balance as a yank pulled her in. Looking up into a wide-open mouth, she fought to keep her eyes from rolling back in response to the emanating smell. She regained her balance and swung forward and away before he could master his depth perception.

Audra shook the funk off and increased the clearance between her and her captive. If she found any mint leaves on their way back, she'd be sure to shove them into his face.

Minty decay.

Finding a rhythm, they started to the laboratory. One upsetting point about not using her biometric reader was that she didn't get to know a name for their journey. Walking through the forest with a zom with no name was not as exciting as it sounded. Names and the nicknames she derived from them made the zoms seem more personable and her days less lonely. She looked at his opposite combover. She was surprised he hadn't lost it. Should she, uh, put it back? Another gasping growl of foul stench told her he'd be OK for another day.

Audra wished she could remember the name of someone in past culture with a combover. That's the name he'd get, but it seemed all her childhood memories of television were fading. One day they'd get back to that, at least re-watching those shows as classics. Maybe they'd eventually make their own again. Audra couldn't imagine a town with resources plentiful enough to support a sitcom. Whatever. Not in her lifetime.

With a few miles under their belt, Audra felt a change in her zom's gait. She could tell a lot by the tautness of the rope, the sway of it, the fetor and noise. Something was different. She turned around then immediately diverted her eyes. She spotted a split tree and led her fellow to it. Pulling his arms through the opening, she wrapped her rope back around the tree and behind him. With his arms secure, he couldn't turn his body. Audra pulled up his pants and tried to tighten his belt, which crumbled in her hands. She pulled out a rope from her bag and tied them up. She didn't have to put up with *that* view the entire run.

Beyond her bodily-fluid soaked zom, she noticed another smell - the distinct smell of burning rubber. Curiosity got the better of her, and since - damn, why couldn't she think of any combover names? - was secure in more ways than one, she investigated. Audra shimmied up a thin pine, the bark scraping her hands. Not the highest view, but she could verify that the scent on the breeze was from miles away. The thick, dark plume rose in the distance, near the highway, probably on the highway.

A car fire? Audra tried to rack her brain for a reason an abandoned car would catch fire on its own, but she knew there had to be a person behind it. Staying hidden was usually a layer of protection against others; whatever their reason for the blaze, they were giving up their location and didn't care.

Audra wasn't too worried about them wandering off the highway and finding her community. Most people who left the highway followed the well-maintained train tracks. It was a golden road to civilization, and it led them to Lysent Corp's string of townships. Her community was hidden deep in the woods.

Her community.

It still felt weird to say that.

But that's what it was. What was first just a laboratory attacked by Lysent had now become a home. They had even named it. If by naming it, you meant they started calling it by the name on the industrial park sign. Osprey Point. Audra had never seen an osprey there, but whatever; it beat calling it "the lab that's now a community." It was a survivor's refuge with one weird exception. Most of these survivors were not initially survivors. They were infected, cured by the scientists at Osprey Point. She looked down at her bound prize. Curly here would be their newest member.

Audra came down and grabbed a handful of acorns from the neighboring tree. They weren't her favorite, but others liked them. They made good flour for bread, but the "coffee" was particularly disgusting. She put them in her bag along with the other found food. That wasn't her mission out here, but any amount helped.

The sun was no longer climbing. They would not make it back before dark. That was fine. They'd stop to eat and camp. She'd have to trap something moving for him - a small mouse or a squirrel would do the trick. Audra appreciated her timing; they'd arrive at Osprey Point in the morning. She'd be able to drop off, resupply, and head back out. With a day's worth of sunlight, Dwyn or the scientists wouldn't have a reason to keep her.

Audra figured the less involved she appeared at Osprey Point, the less likely it was that Lysent would hurt the community to reach her. Larange Greenly, CEO of Lysent, hated what Audra was doing and what she knew, but she didn't appear willing to wage war over her yet, despite her continued stunts.

To appease her friends, she left some things there and claimed a bed-thing. She regularly returned. But still she spent more nights out in the woods in her pop-up tent than in the confines of the fences, and ate most of her meals by a small grate over a fire rather than in the mess hall. Although often out of its range, the radio they shoved into her bag reminded her she hadn't traded much when she got rid of Lysent. She was still out in the woods, capturing zoms, just for a different community. At least this one didn't dangle her sister's life in front of her like a carrot on a stick.

She stayed to keep an eye on Lysent and wait for her chance to destroy them. Once Lysent was shut down with no chance of resurrection, and Greenly was dead for all the things she had done, then Audra would leave. She'd see what else was out there. She'd bring the antidote farther north or west and see more than live oaks and pines and damn mosquitoes.

She slapped at one. She and her zom together emitted that much more carbon dioxide to draw the buggers. And they preferred her fresh blood over the zom's once they arrived. Audra pulled on a long-sleeve shirt and wrapped a cloth around her neck, despite the warm late summer. One bit the high of her cheek. They were insatiable today. She muddied her face. She felt uncomfortable, but at least she was no longer getting chewed up. Not getting destroyed by insects was one thing she missed about modern civilization. She hoped bored survivors would fix that before reviving sitcoms.

With her coverings in place, she looked back - her new friend was now receiving the brunt of the attack. The thought of applying mud to his body made her sick; she decided against it. His kind had spent years trying to bite humans, infecting them. He could get a taste of his own medicine for the evening. When they stopped for the night, they'd get a good smoky fire going and get a breather from the bugs. A good fire, maybe a mouse for her, a rabbit for her friend, a nice sleep. Then they'd be on their way in the sunshine with renewed energy. Maybe he could even run. They'd get there in half the time. Today she'd had one goal. And now, it'd be a good night. Audra smiled and pulled along her new friend. He pulled up closer. Oh yeah, some mint... that'd make it better.

CHAPTER TWO
OSPREY POINT

Little creatures scurried in their wake as Audra and Curly ran for most of the morning. Only her zombie anchor slowed her pace in the soft sunshine and cool breeze that swept through the colored leaves. Before Audra was ready, she caught sight of the gray chain link fences surrounding Osprey Point, and the two guards who stood above the front gate in the scaffolding Ryder had built for them. Someone was on watch twenty-four hours a day. The gate was reinforced with metal paneling, something they hoped to eventually do with the rest of their perimeter. For now, they lined the interior of the fence with old vehicles. It shrank their livable space, but also helped to prevent the fence from bowing if a horde were to come through. The two men equipped with bows, arrows and baseball caps waved to Audra, grimaced at the sight of her find, and then covertly rock-paper-scissored to see who would climb down and escort their guest.

Audra thanked the loser, Branson. His blue eyes twinkled with humor at being caught. He fingered his long brown hair behind his ears before falling in behind the duo. Audra began her hero's walk inside the industrial park, which had taken on new life. Every building was in use - for food, sleeping, living. Real living. They had awakened everyone they could in the business park, finding scientists, maintenance workers, office workers - those who previously worked at Osprey Point were now citizens of Osprey Point. She got lots of smiles and greetings from faces she barely recognized now. Satomi did an excellent job patching people up. And with color to their skin, hair regrowing, and a smile on their lips, it was impossible to recall each of them. Audra returned the smiles, then laughed when they caught sight of her prize and gagged.

The industrial park's asphalt was dusty and dry, weeds cracked through, but the one-story buildings that scattered and connected were built well. The roofs were lined with solar panels, although their ability to store power was limited. The power was mostly used for group work - medical, scientific, and cooking purposes. It wasn't perfect, but it was home for many survivors.

The center held a small plaza with a defunct fountain, the mess hall, the laboratory, and the medical office. Audra turned toward the medical office. The windows were curtained from the inside for privacy. Audra opened the door to its high-traffic carpet and front lobby, which had been stripped of anything comfortable to sit on. All the furniture had been moved into private residences. She peeked her head into the other half of the office. More carpet and three empty stretchers lay in a row with office cubicle partitions to separate the treatment areas. The other side of the room had a long counter with a sink, and shelves stocked full of odds and ends. At the end of the room stood a large metal table, used for office work or surgeries, depending on the day.

She pulled her keep into the office and found Satomi with her head in a cabinet, organizing her supplies.

*   *   *

Satomi pulled her head out of the cabinet when she heard the door creak open. She'd thought she had another box of adhesive tape hidden in there, but no luck. Satomi brightened at the sight of Audra - it was curing day. Audra pulled on her leash. Satomi cringed at the thought of a person on a leash but didn't know how else Audra would manage. She cringed again when she saw her patient.

That amount of skin grafting would not be easy.

"Oh, the poor man. Did you recover his scalp?"

"What? Oh, it's on this side," said Audra, maneuvering the patient. "It's flopped over a bit."

Having the headpiece would make the procedure much simpler. No skin graft needed. "I'll clean and stitch that up before he comes to. Will you find me some volunteers?"

"Yeah, sure. Probably a good idea," she said as she tied the patient's leash to a safety railing by the metal table. Audra left to find some able hands. Satomi cleared the table of her notes and the depleted supply of Lidocaine from this morning's tooth extraction. She pulled her long jet-black hair into a tall bun to keep it out of the way.

Eager to treat both virus and injuries, Satomi didn't waste any time, but rather gave the patient a visual exam as she waited. She then tried to take a pulse, but he swung his head toward her and she decided to wait for others.

Still, she was happy it was curing day, another person to awaken and give a brand-new life. If it was up to her, she'd cure everyone as quickly as possible, but she understood the balance between having enough resources for those already in their community and adding more mouths to feed.

Before administration of the antiviral, she needed to clean and stitch his scalp. The procedure would be quite extensive and any trapped infection would kill him, so anesthetic antibiotics were a must. If she felt his prognosis was acceptable then she'd give him the antiviral to awaken him. In a process Satomi didn't quite understand, the virus protected the brains and bodies. Things that would kill uninfected humans somehow had less impact on infected individuals. Satomi had once treated a long-ago burst appendix in a patient, clearing out the debris and stitching him up. He was fine; the uninfected would not have survived so long. Satomi made sure to give each infected a thorough examination, and treat any possible issues before the awakening process removed the protective nature of the virus. Otherwise, the bodies would quickly succumb to whatever ailed them - mostly infections from injuries. It's like the bodies were on ice - everything slowed, including impending deaths.

Gordon and Dwyn arrived together with heavy leather chaps and jackets to assist with patient positioning.

"EW!" called out Dwyn when he saw the patient's flapping headpiece. His dimples, bright eyes, and constant commentary never hid his emotions. He was taller than Gordon but didn't add grace to his height. Gordon was more professional and made no comment, much to Satomi's appreciation. Although his time infected had slowed his aging, Gordon was still older than she was. He had strong angular features which dwarfed the thin-framed woman's glasses on his face.

The two approached the patient. Gordon bear-hugged him from behind, trying his best to not get a face full of head injury. Dwyn pulled the patient's arms out straight toward Satomi. Satomi set to work quickly, knowing that their hold could be temporary. She didn't have any inhalational anesthetics in her office's supply, so anesthesia would have to be given intravenously, which required finding a vein on patients who were not only dehydrated and sick, but also wouldn't stay still. She put a tourniquet on the bicep and cleaned the lower arm with alcohol and a rag, removing much of the grime to get a better view. Satomi saw her potential target. She slapped at it deftly with her hand before warning her friends of the impending sharp near them. Satomi stuck the patient and the vein rolled a bit (along with the entire arm), but Satomi was used to hitting a moving target. She stuck her tongue out just a bit between her teeth as she navigated around.

A spot of blood appeared within the plastic. Bingo. She secured it with tape as quickly as she could, balancing conservation of supplies and really not wanting to do another IV because this one was pulled out. She grabbed her precious bottle of Propofol they had found in their last supply run of the hospital and, eyeing his weight, gave him a hopefully appropriate dose. At one point, her office had made use of a bathroom scale. It had informed them all the residents were medically underweight, then it was broken shortly thereafter in a scuffle between infected and handler. She had put the replacement low on her wish list.

Her patient slowly stopped fighting, and then Dwyn and Gordon were trying to keep him up rather than keeping him from escaping. They pulled him onto the table as Satomi readied the flexible plastic intubation tube. She tried not to think about its prior uses. Previous single-use items were now used until failure. She had cleaned it out, and technically, it wasn't supposed to be sterile, but it still felt wrong. She got above the patient, still avoiding the wound, and tilted the patient's chin back. First the blade of the laryngoscope, then the tube followed. With the tube's cuff inflated to keep it in place and Dwyn using the self-inflating bag to control the patient's breathing, Satomi scrubbed her hands and began as quickly as possible. She could give him more Propofol in smaller doses to keep him under, but the faster she performed the procedure, the more anesthetic they would have for someone else.

"What did Audra name him?" asked Dwyn, ever curious about Audra as he counted to six under his breath before giving the bag another slow squeeze.

"Curly."

"She's not been very creative lately," he admitted.

"I'd name him Homer, after that old cartoon," said Gordon, before putting the stethoscope up to his ears and pumping up the blood pressure cuff. Satomi surmised Gordon was connecting the infected's injury with the combover of that character. But it wasn't their place to name him. He was a person. He always had been.

If the two men had continued their chatter, Satomi didn't notice. She became lost in her work. She cleared the wound with loads of homemade normal saline and another formerly-disposable bulb syringe. With her sterile tools, she pulled the scalp back into place and began her stitching.

Satomi remembered too late that she should have brought in one of her assistants to watch and learn. Gordon and Dwyn were part of the core team, and she had gotten used to their help. But if some of the new citizens could take on some of these duties, then perhaps she could return to the laboratory. She hadn't even entered the lab in the last couple of weeks. It seemed having a community meant needing a full-time medical doctor - although she hated to admit it. From sprained ankles to toothaches, it was all on her. When she wasn't treating, she was preventing. Illnesses could sweep quickly through their tight quarters and decimate their antibiotic supply. Now, she used a lot of herbal remedies to supplement or to curb sickness before it required traditional drugs. She wasn't sure whether she was a modern doctor or an apothecary at times. Perhaps they were one and the same.

It didn't take but a couple of smaller boluses of Propofol to keep him settled for the duration of the procedure. Gordon had managed to push an entire bag of IV fluid. The patient's skin was already beginning to look less gray, and the veins on his face receded a bit in the returning color of his cheeks. She'd try to give him another half bag of fluid before he woke up and pulled out the IV. Then if all looked all right, he'd get a dose of the antiviral. Often it took a series of doses, but eventually normal brain function would return.

Together they transferred the patient onto the third stretcher from the door. Gordon and Dwyn secured him with wrist and ankle restraints. Satomi continued using the bag to oxygenate him until he woke, then she deflated the cuff and pulled the intubation tube. She'd check its integrity and wash it again. Eventually he'd really awaken and tell them his name.

Satomi would bet a bag of prepared normal saline that it wasn't Curly.

CHAPTER THREE
AUDRA'S SECRET

Audra was on her way to the mess hall for a second breakfast when a young woman with spiky brown hair bounced over to her. She had a bright speck that decorated her tiny nose. Earrings lined one ear. The jewelry and her bright eyes just accentuated her fairy-like qualities, petite but tough. Her bright smile took over half of her face, and Audra couldn't help but be pulled into her office for a talk. It was always good to see Ryder.

They shared a long hug before Ryder pulled around to the other side of her desk which was covered with a bunch of schematics, measurements, and sketches. They were scattered in a mess that Audra couldn't decipher. More papers had crept their way onto the walls, secured this way and that. Not by tape. Tape was in short supply. While Audra had never thought much of the rundown business park, Ryder's vision, keen engineering mindset, and wicked hard work had created a sanctuary. And, as much as this office didn't look it - it was the office of the mayor.

"I want to do a council meeting tomorrow, since you're in town," she said, pulling herself onto her desk, sitting cross-legged on the mess. She looked down at a sketch that looked like a silo, frowned, and grabbed a pencil and scribbled a couple of numbers.

"Can't we do it today? I'd like to not stay," muttered Audra, not really wanting to elaborate. Audra didn't agree with the added complication of council meetings, much less them actually meeting. She had often voiced that concern in the council meetings, much to everyone's frustration.

Ryder glanced up, her eyebrows also rising.

"Satomi is going to want to monitor her patient... About the meeting, I want to nominate you as mayor during the meeting."

"Hell no." She crossed her arms over her chest.

"Look, I'm great at the town-building stuff. It's the rest of this leadership thing - I've no idea what I'm doing. I'm an engineer, not a mayor," Ryder confided in her.

Audra disagreed. Ryder was doing an amazing job creating a workable infrastructure with a population that was only growing. She had set up a water filtration system and was even trying her hand at designing the farms for efficiency. It made Audra's head spin - the way she balanced immediate needs with what was best for the future. She understood Ryder's desire to slough away the politics, but what she was actually asking, Audra wanted no part of.

"Audra, I don't think anyone's more capable than you. And it wouldn't be just you - the others are a big help. I'd be a big help."

"I wouldn't make a good leader. All I want is to wake up the sick and tear down Greenly. That's not much of a plan or a future. You need me out there pulling in more people. You can glean leaders from the cured."

It was hard to argue with it, but it was also just a really good excuse to not be a part of civilization. They were lucky she didn't run off in the first place, that she returned here as a home base.

Hell, maybe this was Ryder's and the council's secret plan to root her. It wouldn't be their first.

They were interrupted by someone coming in with a question about the storage silo. Nobody knew what they were doing except Ryder, and even she just went by principles she had learned in engineering, not because she had ever built a silo before. Ryder recited the new number she had written down in anticipation of their question, and they headed out. Audra didn't even know the person's name. Marla, maybe? And that's why they needed Ryder. Ryder connected with everyone. Even when they were first journeying to Osprey Point, she'd kept up morale and confidence despite not knowing what they would find there. Audra did not have the affability or patience for such tasks.

"I wish you'd think on it more. I don't feel comfortable here. I was happy to lead *us* - not an entire community. If not you, then someone."

Perhaps she was serious. Maybe she'd talk to Satomi and get her feel for it. Satomi, now regulated to full-time medical doctor (although Audra didn't dare tell her that) was Ryder's best friend. She'd know better what Ryder really wanted. Audra made a note to do that in the next couple of days.

Until then, to appease Ryder, she replied, "Yes, I'll think about who else could lead, but, you'll have to give us some time. You're doing great."

*   *   *

After a second breakfast in the mess hall, Audra raced to the refitted office building to find her room in the maze of hallways. Audra imagined from the amount of paperwork they cleared from there, it had been an insurance office, but she also never bothered to look at the legal-ese to confirm. She was given a small room toward the front - easy escape.

She began swapping out things in her bag. The morning had gotten away from her and she wasn't sure if she'd be fast enough.

She wasn't fast enough.

"Where are you going now?" asked Dwyn, his curly-haired head popping through the doorway of her little room. Damn, she should have shut the door. Were they really done with Curly already?

"Back out. I have the rest of the day to find someone else. How is Curly?" she asked, trying to keep the topic on zoms and not her or him, or worse, her and him.

"He is resting. *You* could *also* rest," he suggested as he did so against her door frame. His shoulders had gotten even broader, she thought. She dismissed the thought.

"I rested last night nearby." Not addressing the real point. "I'll check the snares before I head out."

"You're coming back tonight, though, right?"

"Why?" She slung her bag onto her shoulder.

"The council meeting tomorrow."

Shit. Ryder had already told him.

"When you're back, can we hang out?" he asked with some trepidation, then proceeded to slip off the door frame. Audra gave a giggle, much to her aggravation.

She enjoyed his friendship, but things had gotten complicated. The kiss. Then, she had been rather unguarded and emotional at the falls when he'd arrived and helped her bury her sister, but she couldn't stay that person. And besides, what was the point of owning an anchor? She'd be leaving here soon enough. It was easier to just... not.

"No, I don't think so."

His eyes darkened a bit at the invitation's decline.

"Give yourself permission to be here, Audra," he said as he walked away.

He could take a hike. She didn't owe him her company. Audra stomped through the maze of office halls to find the stockpile of clothes that people could pull from. She needed some new socks to compensate for the fact that she needed new shoes. *What did he know?* Her thoughts raced. Becoming permanent residents and setting down roots in a town was a dream for her and her sister. Belinda craved people and attention and gave love freely. She needed a town. To live here without her... Audra wasn't sure she wanted to.

With a quick nod from her to the guard, the gate wheeled to let her out. She ran out into the golden hues and burnt coppers of fall without looking back at the dusty overcrowded community. To live there and love there was for Dwyn, for Belinda. She didn't need it.

*　　*　　*

The crunching of the leaves underneath her feet reminded her they were running out of time to make provisions and preparations for winter. It could come fast. It could also leave again for another scorching summer-like day. The south was weird like that. Audra didn't know how those up north survived their intense winters, but at least winter was assured.

The oak trees were dropping their green acorns. Most of them had sunk into soft ground and she padded her way through. Occasionally one would catch underneath her feet and threatened to roll her onto hard dirt and roots. She laughed and stepped with fast short beats.

Audra ran past the stretch of planted mulberry trees, which had given all they had to offer weeks ago. Rumor had it that some of the fruit might reappear as wine in a couple of months. One could only hope. Audra observed that the hickory nut trees also needed a rest from hungry fingers. If she thought a single runner needed obscene amounts of food, it was nothing compared to a hungry settlement. Audra recalled Larange Greenly's rants about the difficulties of keeping her towns fed, despite their resources and stockpiles. Ryder had many systems in place for their community as well. Still, Audra wondered what they would do when things got scarce. If things got really bad.

The bleating and commotion filled her ears before she met the third snare. When she arrived to leaves flying, her excitement faded into a bit of sadness as she could almost taste the young doe's fear. Small. She could handle it herself. Audra pulled the magic out of her bag - a concoction in darts - a joint project by medical Satomi and engineering Ryder. Audra was careful not to touch the end. She was no match for something that could take out a deer. Rather than take aim at the flailing, she sat down and waited. The deer's coat was splotched in transition from summer to winter coat. It panted and writhed, but she knew it would eventually pause in its frantic motion to look at her. She'd already have aim and be ready to shoot. It would take a couple of good hits, but it was worth it.

Pop.

Got her.

And one more.

She took a few moments to let the sedation settle before unhooking the deer from the snare and setting ropes upon it. The doe was a heavy thing, but Audra was a stubborn thing. She braced her feet and found the starting momentum to get her onto the wrinkled patched tarp, and the tarp moving. Occasionally, the doe gathered enough strength to attempt another self-rescue. Its limbs kicked and bucked and more than once Audra had to let go of the rope. She'd rather pull zombies. They were a much more cooperative field partner.

A sense of uneasiness settled over the space between her heart and her stomach. Audra swiveled her head to look while still trying to maintain forward momentum. It was difficult to sense another presence in the woods with the deer so close. Maybe Dwyn had suspected she'd found something in the snares and had come to help. But he'd be coming up the path, which Audra had just reached, and there was no one in sight. On the worn single track, she dug her feet into the dirt and they picked up additional speed. She told herself that it would build strength in her legs. Maybe she should have let such a young doe go, but she needed it. Not to feed her people, but to feed her next people. Their turn.

Audra wasn't sure if she kept the corral of uncured a secret because of the surrounding politics or because she was ashamed of it. Osprey Point was founded on a cure for all. No payment. No indentured servitude. You were cured and that was it. End of story. However, it turned out it wasn't that simple.

Each person they awakened from their zombie state had only the rags on her back, heartbreaking confusion, and a disturbing absence of survival skills. A "catch and release" program would prove lethal, or at least counterproductive in terms of reinfection. By some degree, they were responsible for each life recovered. They taught each one to forage for edibles, how to hunt, and how to keep sheltered and warm - Audra recalled Dwyn's dismal attempts to build a fire prior to her teaching him. How Dwyn had survived without that skill boggled Audra's mind. *Where had he been?* But she didn't dare ask when she refused to share anything of her own.

Despite skills taught, everyone remained firmly within the fences, content to stay in Osprey Point. And a community filling to the brim meant a backlog of people to awaken. A backlog just in this small part of a Southern state alone. Audra hated Lysent, but they were right about one thing. You can't wake them all up at once. You need infrastructure. You need a system. And until then, you need a corral.

Dwyn and Ryder were the only other two who knew about the corral. Even among three, it remained a point of contention. It was too close. It was insecure. It was an accidental herd waiting to happen. Yes, yes, yes, it was all those things. A corral did nothing good for the zombies within or the humans nearby. After much debate, it was decided they would funnel any secured materials or time into expanding the community working toward eliminating the corrals once and for all.

The deer had given up its noise by the time they pulled up to the corral. Her head and neck rested sadly on the tarp. A rusted trailer, long emptied of its goods, stood in a cleared field - someone's loot a long-time past. Audra could hear them shuffling inside. She tied the deer's legs and hoisted it up with the pulley system that Ryder had built. After tying it off, she climbed up to meet it. The zoms could smell the fear and the meat. Their scuffling rolled into a frenzy. She dragged the deer to the rusted portion of the roof that had been peeled open with great manual labor. In one last attempt to save its life, the doe flopped and threw Audra dangerously off balance. The metal near the edge bent with her weight but did not give this time. Audra sat on her rear and scooted away before pushing the deer into the groaning darkness below.

Audra lay back and settled onto the warm metal of the corral. Her body vibrated with the activity therein. She listened to the scream and ripping of flesh. *What sort of life was this?* She'd give herself permission to live when the world was worth living in. She rolled off the corral and headed back toward Osprey Point.

CHAPTER FOUR
THE STRANGER

When Audra came out of the woods and onto the asphalt, her stride opened up into a sprint to the front gate. Ziv jumped down and managed to slide the gate open just in time as Audra came bounding through. She skidded to a stop with a smile.

Two scientists manned the gates, the easy shift that ended with the fading light. Ziv, with his long straggly beard that overtook his thin frame, was one of them.

"Who's next on shift?" she asked. She hoped she had timed it perfectly to avoid another awkward encounter with Dwyn.

"Marcos and Gordon," Ziv reported.

Audra gave him a pat on the shoulder as thanks as she began to slow her breathing. She'd look for them in the mess hall. They were probably preparing for their shift, and if not, Audra could use a snack. She jumped onto the short walls of the fountain and skipped along its border.

Previously the mess hall was the designated corral in the industrial park. Now, the front room served as a place to gather and eat if one so desired. And one mostly did, since their rooms were isolated and boring. The back room served as a food pantry and limited kitchen.

Their diet was primarily a mixture of farmed, found, and hunted food. Late summer berries gave way to mulberry leaves and dandelion greens. These were supplemented with what meat they might have on hand, typically made into a stew to make it go further. They also traded for Lysent food blocks with some townships that were willing to keep it on the down low.

Audra entered the mess hall, which had a collection of eclectic tables and chairs, including the large conference table from the laboratory. She spotted Marcos first. His head was bowed, leaving his dark hair swinging low and covering his face. He was lining up his berries in size order on his plate, or maybe it was in order of ripeness - Audra couldn't tell.

"Yo Marcos," she said swinging her leg over the bench across from him. She grabbed a handful of berries from the bowl on the table as well.

Marcos looked over at her haphazard way of eating berries. She dared to put more than one into her mouth at a time. He disapproved by saying nothing in return. While amusing, she knew that his orderliness balanced the other scientists' absentminded messiness in the laboratory.

"Can I take your guard shift?" she asked.

"Uh, sure, but it's a double... I traded with Dwyn, something about he had plans."

Audra smiled at Dwyn's failed attempt. Her plan had

become ironically perfect as long as Dwyn did not catch whiff of it. Then, she'd be stuck in awkward silence hoping for a zombie attack just to ease the tension.

"No worries. I got it."

Audra sat next to Gordon, whose thin-framed woman's glasses barely fit on his nose. Audra still had not mustered the courage to tell him what had happened to his original glasses. These did match his prescription, allowing him to work unimpeded in the laboratory and as guard, but they for sure didn't match his face.

They both sat cross-legged on the scaffolding and looked into the dark distance.

"How's the search going?" she asked.

Gordon had a daughter and an ex-wife he hadn't seen since before the outbreaks. She worked for Lysent; maybe they had survived. Eliza would be eight years old now.

Gordon scoffed. "I don't know. Still going, I guess." His voice broke at the end.

Audra wasn't sure what to say. She had known it was a long shot. She should never have scanned his DNA with her reader. She had told herself that there was no harm in trying, but there was harm in the false hope it had given him.

Audra had scraped the reader as lightly against his shoulder as she could, but the scientist had winced all the same. Audra had always wondered how much it hurt. It didn't bother most of her targets. Turns out, that was because their bodies were dealing with too much internal pain. Nothing external signaled as loudly, possibly why they kept going even when falling apart or torn apart by physical weapons. Nothing told them to stop.

BING

"What does it say? What does that mean?" Gordon had asked from his perch on the metal table in Satomi's office.

A single *BING*. Audra had known what that meant right away, but she'd pretended to read the display anyway. In her tagging life, almost no money had ever come from a single *BING*.

Inquired, but no deposit paid.

The logistics of finding the family, the family still wanting the individual and suddenly having the means to cover the expense? It always meant milling around until you gave up and found a better zom. Gordon had waited for her answer.

"It means 'Inquired'. At some point, someone asked about you."

"They're alive." His voice had rasped with all the possibilities. He'd jumped up as if he had somewhere to go.

"Gordon, it doesn't mean that at all," Audra had said, touching his arm to slow him. "It means at some point, someone looked you up. The tagging program has been running for nearly four years now. Your family could have checked and then moved on. And to be honest, I bet Greenly inquired for all the scientists in this laboratory once she realized its strategic importance."

"But if it was my family, they'll notify them now, right?"

"They're supposed to. But, I imagine all employees of this facility are marked. They're not going to help us."

"Then, I'll look on my own. This is hope."

Audra had kept to herself what the single *BING* meant to her.

"Do you think they'd head south or north?" she asked

now, hating herself for encouraging him.

"North, definitely. She had family up there."

Audra nodded into the deep darkness. Gordon ran his hand through his hair and adjusted his glasses.

There wasn't much hope, but Audra knew she would search too if she were in his place. Besides, what else was there to do but look?

*　　*　　*

After a few hours of sleep and the promise she'd return in time for the meeting, Audra was back out with the coolness of the morning. She couldn't comprehend how anyone could stay cooped up in that industrial park. The padding of her feet and the soft dew greeted her like an old friend. Soon the dew dried, leaving the crunching rhythm of fall.

A rhythm that was being cut into.

Audra paused, but all of the crunching did not. She looked ahead toward the noise that approached and the figure that made it. Audra pulled out her knife and held it ready. Who was here so close to Osprey Point?

The figure did not change pace, so Audra stood and waited. It was a zombie. Or was it? Its feet shuffled but its back was straight as if the infection had started from the bottom and hadn't quite reached its way to the top. Even from this distance, she observed its drained color, that sandy gray that overtook flesh - a veil over humanity. It had no damage, no gouges, no weapons protruding from its torso. As much as it looked like a zom in excellent condition, Audra's mind refused to accept it.

Something was off.

Its movements weren't quite right. Its limbs moved with more coordination than what felt familiar. Audra swore it was making small corrections around obstacles. She watched its left foot rise slightly higher, avoiding a root.

As he got closer, Audra could see that he could have been a healthy survivor this morning. He was built. His muscles hadn't atrophied. His spine didn't droop in odd directions. He had all his hair, unlike scalped Curly.

He wore a loose burlap sack, not something people would choose for themselves. Audra remembered the dagger in her hand as her eyes searched the forest for the wardrobe designer. No one else around. None of this felt good or safe. He hadn't seen her yet, even though she was close to his direct trajectory.

"Hey you!" she dared call out.

He looked at her. Audra expected him to attack. She waited for him to spring, launch himself, and reach out with his strong arms. He was much taller than she was and she wondered how much his improved condition would be to her disadvantage. But he just looked at her, then turned his head ever so slightly back to its forward position as he continued his march.

"I'm talking to you! Are you OK?"

He did not answer.

A zombie that did not want to bite people? Or a trick, a man in disguise?

Audra wasn't sure how close to let him approach.

"Look, you can't go that way. I need you to go back where you came from. I've claimed all these woods. It's my hunting ground. You can't get to wherever you're going from here. You're going to have to go somewhere else and start from there."

No response. Not even a side-eye glance at her joke. Whether he knew it or not, he was making a beeline to Osprey Point. Maybe he'd keep walking right into one of their walls. Audra wasn't sure what the deal was, but she needed to redirect him like she'd redirected hundreds of zoms before.

He was almost to her and Audra could see the dark gray of his eyes. No one could fake that. He wasn't there. This wasn't a disguise; this was him. Whatever *him* was. Audra shoved his left arm. His right leg came out to stop him from falling. It was a reflex but usually not a successful one for his kind. He adjusted his trajectory ever so much to correct for her efforts.

If his instincts weren't strong enough to chase her on sight, then she'd have to become more enticing. What else drew zombies in?

Audra cringed. Blood. Blood drew zombies in. The smell, the sight, the crying that often accompanied it. She looked around, even though she knew it would do no good. There were no convenient animals or reservoirs of blood to grab on a whim. The only thing that had delicious blood was her. She looked down at her dagger, which she hoped she had cleaned more recently than she recalled. The zom brushed past her. She gave a little slice to her hand near her thumb before she could change her mind. He didn't immediately turn around so she recovered the distance. In a move that she considered only as she got there, she offered the knife with the blood on it rather than her bloodied hand. His head turned at the smell and his lip sneered upward. She had him with the scent of blood. But how much of him did she have? Not enough - something still drove him forward. He did not stay.

Audra pulled on his arm. When she refused to let go, a fist swung toward her. She let go before his fist followed through. Instead, she ran in front of him and dived for his legs. He did nothing to avoid her and fell over. She escaped him and he reoriented himself to his original direction, the direction to Osprey Point, before pulling himself up. She kicked him in the back, causing him to fall again. He just moved to get back up.

What was wrong with him? What was this?

She would not let him reach her community. He was a threat, an unknown infection. She pulled out the rope from her bag, the second time in two days, and swung it onto her shoulder. She'd kick him down again, but this time in a more opportune place.

She waited until he neared the right tree, then she drove her foot into the back of one of his knees. Down he went. Audra worked quickly but carefully. She wasn't sure what he would resort to when he realized he was being subdued. She dragged him close to the tree. So far so good. She tied the rope around him and then around the tree. Around and around it went. The zom began fighting at this point. Pulling, struggling, trying to get his hands free. He finally resorted to opening his mouth to bite.

Audra secured him with a knot and looked around to get her bearings. She would bring Satomi and the scientists here to examine him and treat him if they could.

She thought of the cure stashed away in her bag that Dwyn had given her. No. She didn't even know if it would work, or what he had. She would save hers for a rainy day. For *that* rainy day.

Audra started off in the same trajectory as the zom intended. Was it a coincidence that he was heading in the direction of Osprey Point, or something Audra shouldn't ignore? She was lucky to have found him. If they awakened him, would he be able to explain how he'd gotten sick and with what? He couldn't have cared less that she was there. Audra wondered how the virus spread if insatiable hunger didn't drive him. Maybe he was a one-off; Audra hoped he was a one-off.

Audra raced through the gates to Satomi's office. She'd oversee the treatment, possibly in the lab. The conference room hadn't been used for quarantine for so long.

Satomi was seeing someone on a stretcher behind one of the movable walls. Audra shifted from one foot to the other waiting impatiently. Yes, he was tied to a tree, but something felt off. Audra wanted to know what was going on. She knew zombies. Even if Satomi and the others refused to call them that, Satomi knew them too. This wasn't a zombie. This was something else. And the sooner they figured it out, the better.

Right as Audra was considering interrupting the office visit - probably some ingrown toenail or toothache - something interrupted her.

"HEY OOO!" called someone from outside the fences.

CHAPTER FIVE
JACK & JILL

"We'd like to talk!" they said unnecessarily. Of course, they wanted to talk; otherwise they'd have attacked already. About what and on whose terms, was the concern. The infected in the woods quickly disappeared from her mind as she peered through the reinforced front gates to see an armored man and woman with a handful of support behind them.

"Invite them in?" asked a squeaky Ryder, sidling up to Audra. Lionel, one of the guards on duty, had found her.

"No. You don't want them to gain any easy knowledge about us. You want them to suspect that we are more powerful, more numerous, and more guarded than we are. You want them to doubt whatever moves they make," Audra said in hushed voices to her leader, her eyes glued to the group outside.

"Oh, right..." Ryder said. In a louder voice, she said, "let's meet them outside the gates where our guards can watch overhead."

By this point, Dwyn had emerged from the mess hall to join them. Others flooded from the community buildings and funneled into the residence quarters. At least they'd be out of the way.

As the gate opened, the doors further revealed the duo. The woman had long, blond hair that swept around her shoulders and into a braid that went down to her waist. She wore flexible leather armor tucked into her boots, and a sliver of skin showed that her suit was two pieces at the waist. Her wrists, hands, and neck – all popular and vulnerable spots for zombie bites – were covered and guarded. She stood of equal height to the man, whose blond hair was spiked with gel and styling. He wore heavy strips of leather on his forearms and on his shoulders. He carried a short, pointed sword and she carried a glimmering hand-axe. Their weapons showed that they liked close combat, and their being alive provided evidence of their ability.

The two looked similar, maybe siblings or just that weird thing where people start to look like each other when they are in relationships. Either way, it was obvious by their body posture that they were the power couple of the group: clean, pretty, and confident. The others stood a few feet behind them, their hands on weapons as well.

"Hello!" said friendly Ryder, although her voice wavered just a bit at the end. "I'm Ryder. This is Audra and Dwyn."

The woman raised her eyebrows and the man made no gesture. For people who wanted to talk, they were not quick to do so. The pair sized up the crew visually before the man spoke.

"I'm Jack. She's Jill."

Ryder held out her hand to shake, but Jack and Jill made no movement to do the same.

"Where are you from?" asked Ryder as she lowered her unreceived hand.

"New Tennessee. We came to escape the winter. We like it warmer, although we imagine your zoms stay active year-round?"

"They slow down up there? We haven't really noticed a difference. Well, they get a bit smelly during the summer," remarked Dwyn.

Jill giggled, but it was a bit of a dark humor giggle. Audra didn't trust it or Jill.

"*New* Tennessee?" asked Audra.

"Yes. I guess it was Virginia? answered Jack. "But a group migrated up there from Tennessee and renamed it for their own."

So, there were more survivors, at least on this side of the Mississippi and south of the Mason-Dixon line.

"So, this place," Jack started. "Looks like it used to be an industrial park - offices and such."

Ryder nodded.

"Did you wake up anyone from here?" he asked casually.

"Yes, we sure did."

Were they trying to reunite with family?

"Any scientists?"

Ryder answered before Audra could signal her to shut up. "Oh yes!"

"Good. We want them. Doctors too."

"What?" choked Ryder at their demand.

Jack and Jill gave a cold stare. Their minions behind them tensed and seemed to grow larger.

"We won't give you people," Audra said, her patience

thinning. Dwyn touched her wrist, a sign to be careful. Audra pulled her arm away. She was not going to be cajoled by him out here. Or anywhere. She shot him daggers and he backed off.

"We're stronger than you," said Jill simply.

"Then there must be more of you?" suggested Audra. "Because you're just five here and you don't look any stronger."

Jill laughed at her, like Audra had just told a joke.

"You'd be surprised," she murmured, "but yes, there are more. We could take over, but we might not want to. So, what do you have?"

"Audra's right, we don't deal in people. But if you're interested in scientists, we might be one step ahead of you." Audra closed her eyes and deeply inhaled as she listened to Ryder's mistake. "We have an antiviral for the pandemic. It works. We can trade it with you."

"So, you *do* have scientists. Good ones too. Bring them out to trade."

This wasn't working.

"We'll do no such thing," said Ryder, crossing her arms.

Jack and Jill turned heel and ominously walked away.

"Well good riddance," muttered Dwyn.

As the duo reached the forest line, Jill raised her arm. With the snap of her fingers, dark figures emerged from the brush in a long neat line. Audra flashed back to Greenly's attack with shredded and weathered zoms. These were not those. They walked purposefully rather than shuffling. Like the zom she'd met in the woods, these looked strong. It would be unlike anything they'd ever encountered before, and Audra suddenly wished they had done more to fortify their community.

Audra noticed the zoms all carried weapons, despite

the assurance that they could not possibly use them. They were too clumsy and uncoordinated as zombies. Was it just a scare tactic?

She wouldn't believe it if she hadn't seen it with her own eyes. One of the zombies, a man with a rectangular face and a crew cut pulled a grenade from his belt, released the pin, and rolled the explosive along the ground ahead of their attack.

Audra and her friends scattered to avoid it.

"Is this real?" asked Ryder as the grenade came short of them and exploded into dust, sticks, and stones. It wasn't the best toss, but the fact that it could happen was amazing in itself.

And they were in danger.

The trio retreated back through the gates, which closed quickly on their tails, no request required. The guards, Marcos and Lionel, were seeing this too. Complex actions from zombies.

"I know you were ordered to come forward, but we don't mean you all any harm," called out Ryder through the gate. A shot in the dark. "We would like to trade. To learn. To understand."

No response. No reaction.

Ryder tried another tactic. "JACK! JILL! Stop this madness! Please, let's work together. Call off your soldiers."

But they did not. They were nowhere to be seen.

Twenty or so encroached. The car-lined chain link fence would hold against twenty zoms. Hell, it would hold against fifty or more, but what kind of attack were they about to meet?

Despite having seen one up close, Audra still didn't believe it. They must be humans posing as zombies to scare them, but Audra could see the purple veins webbing their gray faces. She saw the emptiness in their eyes. And she could see little issues with their stance, their swagger, their facial expressions. They might not be full-fledged zombies, but they weren't full-fledged healthy humans either. They were some hybrid.

Audra called out to Marcos, who had a bow and quiver of arrows. He made eye contact - his eyes were wild with fear and confusion. She motioned to her own shoulder then chose a zom - a half zom? The half zom's hair had been cut short - someone had given him a haircut - and he walked without concern for his wellbeing, as if he didn't understand the significance of enemy lines. Audra wanted Marcos to hit him, but not in the head. Would it slow or stop him? Would it rile the group? Marcos gave a nod and took aim.

The arrow came from above into his shoulder, blasting through his clavicle. His shoulder slumped as he was knocked off balance, but he didn't fall. Anyone would fall. Yet except for the long shaft emerging from his body, there was no other clue that the arrow had hit. She signaled again and another plunged into his chest, missing his heart. There was no evidence of pain, discomfort even, just a distraction - a slowdown. In the realm of weaponization they had all the benefits of zom and human - the ability to follow directions, perform complex movements, and the painlessness and fearlessness of zoms.

She gave permission to let arrows fly.

Regardless, the half zoms reached the fence and began to claw and climb. Audra grabbed several long spears stored near the fence for hordes. She passed them out to Dwyn and Ryder. The zoms moved fast but were not making perfect progress. Audra and her crew stood on the cars and started charging the spears through the fence. It was difficult to get an effective blow through their dense skulls, but strikes to the face or multiple jabs seemed to weaken their grip on the fences. They did not try to avoid the shots, as they were seemingly unaware of weapons, injury, or death. They climbed up and up then fell with the spears.

"Let's save one," whispered Ryder. Ryder was right; Satomi would want to study it. They would need to know if they could be cured. An awakened soldier might tell them what they were and where they were from. *New Tennessee, my ass.*

With just one remaining, Audra signaled to have the gate open. With the creak of the gate, the zom dropped from his position two-thirds up the fence. He hit the ground, planting both feet, his knees bent to soften the landing. It appeared his directive was to enter in the most efficient way possible. When it was easier to walk in, he stopped climbing.

Audra recognized him as he approached the fence. It was the one she had tied up in the woods. So, that was the way they had come. They had found it and untied it. He must have been a scout. Audra kicked herself for not having realized it, but since when were zombies scouts?

Audra and the two gave him a wide berth. She didn't spot any grenades on him, only a knife. He pulled it from its sleeve and stood in a defensive position without approaching them. Maybe he only had orders to enter? Maybe he was waiting for his comrades? Audra was not sure.

Ryder walked into his visual range.

"Hi. I'm sorry we had to hurt your friends. We can't suffer an attack here. Who are you? What is it you want?"

There was no answer, just a blank stare. Brainwashing? Was there a trigger?

"Look," said Dwyn, "we don't want to hurt you. Drop the knife and let's talk. You can be safe here."

Another blank stare. His dark gray eyes barely followed their movements. His mouth hung open slightly, revealing bloody teeth.

Audra sneaked behind in an attempt to disarm him, but as she approached, he swung around and hit her with a strong arm, knocking her off balance. She staggered. Audra realized she had little advantage here. He was a soldier, and Audra was small and used to chasing around dummies. But it didn't matter, this guy had to be taken down. She went in again, but someone pushed her to the side. It was Dwyn. He grabbed the half zom's knife hand and wrestled with it. Audra's eyes flashed with anger at his protective stunt. She pulled herself up and took the opportunity to punch the half zom in the jaw, releasing some of her frustration. The jaw did not give as she had hoped. He was not rotting; he just looked it.

Both Dwyn and the zom ended up on the ground. Audra's vexation melted into worry for Dwyn. Her mom's cut and seeping infection flashed in her mind's eye, making it difficult to see the situation now. Her eyes watered and her heart began to pound from her chest. She pushed forward to Dwyn, trying to distance herself from the memories. Together they pulled the knife from the zom's hand and subdued him.

Audra called for rope. He was a large man and they wouldn't be able to hold him for long. As she called, someone else called, too. Audra looked up at the noise coming from the woods. A snapping. A snapping of many fingers. Audra did not like the sound of this. A goodbye or a hello?

It was a hello.

Another forty zoms came sprinting from the woods.

No longer walking, they took long, fast strides to the fences and gave a jumping start to reach the top. With Audra and Dwyn distracted, their prisoner punched free and ran back to the gate. He began climbing toward the guards who controlled the gate. Damn. Was this their plan all along?

Audra called for her own help. She wanted to hesitate. Her citizens were not fighters. They were just survivors. But they knew the dangers of living out here in the isolation. She stood in the plaza and yelled for others to come with weapons and to fight.

Audra took off to the gate, but the two above waved her off. They could handle this intruder. Arrows came flying into the plaza.

"No! Shoot the ones outside the fences. I'll get this one," Audra called out, pissed that she had fallen for their trap and had let this one in.

How she would handle him, she didn't know. He was bigger and stronger, but she did have his knife and she could run. She sprinted hard and fast and tackled his legs. She sliced into his Achilles tendon, causing his leg to buckle. She cut into the other then pulled high. Audra breathed a sigh of relief as he fell down, the knife landing in the small of his back. Another frantic move left it in his neck. Blood spouted and she rolled off.

But he rolled too. He yanked the knife from his neck and approached Audra with it. He at least swaggered with the blood loss. Audra pulled out her own knife from her belt and hunkered into a protective stance. She watched the blood course. She only had to buy time before he fell again, but that same blood covered her too. Would it make her sick? He charged.

As he leapt, he fell at Audra's feet. Audra saw an arrow in his back from the guards above. She guessed Marcos hadn't believed she had it handled. She was thankful. Had that arrow done him in or just pushed him over? Audra drove her blade where his head and neck met, to be sure.

She found her abandoned spear and turned her attention to the fence. Lionel and Marcos were having little luck keeping all the zoms at bay. Audra stabbed two in the stomach. They gushed like stuck pigs but if the wounds and blood loss slowed them down, it was imperceptibly so. At least the blood made their feet slip on the links of the fence. Audra would have to wait for them to come down, on either side. The barbed wire at the top of the fence was curled to keep out humans but Audra knew it would only tear these zoms. They would be slippery and covered in infectious material when they landed in the plaza.

Audra heard yells from above. Lionel fell from his top spot, an arrow in his chest, and landed on the other side of the fence. Immediately two half zoms leapt upon him and began feasting. An instinct or a command? Numbness swept through Audra as he was torn to bits. Dwyn squeezed her shoulder. This was not the time to freeze.

She called out to Marcos to take cover - a useless command, as he had already done so. She looked behind her and saw a few men timidly coming with kitchen knives. There were only a few to be counted as warriors. Branson came out with a sharpened machete. Tess's white blond hair flashed in the sunlight. She grabbed a spear and began to attack those on the fences. Gordon emerged from the lab with his long knife. He sprinted to the fences and climbed up to meet the zoms at the top.

They were coming over the fences now. They landed firm-footed on the cars, leaving skin and clothes behind. One got caught by his belt and hung there. His head beat against the barbed wires as he tried to fight loose. Blood sprayed and bounced downward. Another approached Audra. This time she was ready. With her spear, she stabbed him in the eye, reaching into the brain. He stopped moving, then crumpled to the ground. Audra shook him loose and turned to find another.

"In the eye!" she yelled. She knew some of the others would not be as skilled, but it was better than stomach stabbing and jugular cuts that only doused everyone with infectious blood. Audra poked another from behind to get him to turn. His face was ripped open but Audra could still see his snarl. Into the eye she went, avoiding his knife swing, which was fairly accurate for his half blindness. Her spear sank farther in as he moved closer to her, jaw snapping as he died. He fell on top of Audra. His bloodied dead weight trapped her. The short spear dug into the ground, blocking one side. As she crawled her way out, she saw.

Ryder had lost her weapon and was frantically tripping backward in an attempt to gain some distance from a half zom about to overtake her. The zom's blade shone and flittered as he quick-stepped his way to her.

Audra pulled her legs out from underneath as she called to Dwyn, "Help Ryder!"

Ryder took a sidestepping dodge from the knife's jab. And another, and another.

Suddenly, Audra saw red and it was not the zom's. She called out. Audra pulled free and ran. She jumped onto the zom's back, anxious to change its direction, focus, target. Ryder held her side and cried, but her eyes remained glued to the scene from the ground. Her shouts brought out Satomi seeking her friend. It was the best thing for Ryder. A medic. Immediately. Audra yanked at the zom's chin, trying to break its neck but not having the leverage. Still, she knocked him off balance and down they went together. Her eyes searched for her spear.

Still in the other zom.

She grabbed a knife from her ankle boot. One to use, one to lose. She pursed her lips and squinted her eyes as tightly as she could without losing sight of her target, and came down on his neck. His jugular spouted, which was enough to distract him as Audra stabbed at his face. She guarded her eyes from the destruction, but she knew it would visit her dreams. Who was he? Audra's tears streamed down her face as he stopped moving. There had to be another way. A less sickening way.

She looked around. She wasn't the only one covered in blood. There were others. And everything was still. The few zoms on the other side of the fence retreated. Some of her comrades lay injured or torn. No sign of the dreaded Jack or Jill.

Satomi and Ryder had disappeared into the medical office but no one looked for Ryder.

They all looked to Audra, who sat atop a man whose face and life she had destroyed.

As the others combed through the bodies for friends and injured, she found a clean spot on her shirt and wiped her face of blood, being careful around her eyes. Infection was possible. And the cure may or may not help.

"Audra?" Dwyn called out from the far side of the fence. "This one is still alive."

CHAPTER SIX
TRIAGE

Satomi couldn't do much in the battle; instead she gathered her triage supplies in the medical office. She sent away the mother and the child she was treating for a splinter. She cleared the area to make way for injuries and called in her volunteers. She'd help the fighters once they arrived here. Until then, she could only sit and watch at the window. And whom she watched most was Ryder.

Her volunteers, two young women, stood in the corner and fidgeted with supplies. Both with sandy brown hair and big blue eyes, looked positively terrified. They whispered to each other as Satomi ignored them. Their fear response was normal. Satomi knew they'd be worthless before they could be useful. It was the same when she had first started. This was a learning experience.

Satomi watched Ryder's spiked brown hair bob up and

down as she dodged enemies. Satomi felt sick to her stomach. It was like watching a movie. She had no control. Her heart lurched forward, urging her to go help her friends. But she knew she could not. They needed fighters and she would not fight. In her medical studies she'd adopted an oath, *Primum non nocere* or "First, do no harm." And it went well past her medical practice. Besides, they needed her here. An injured or dead medic was no good.

Ryder's head went down. Satomi's face smashed involuntarily against the glass and her thin lips contorted in sympathetic fear and pain. She brushed her hair away from her face, and tried to get a better look by pressing even closer to the glass. Ryder was doubled over, holding her side. Was she bit? Stabbed? Satomi couldn't stand it anymore. Her hair swung as pendulums behind her as she threw open the door and ran headlong into the crowd.

When she arrived, she found Ryder's face scrunched in pain but it meant that she was conscious. Ryder's hands held her side. Blood flowed and bubbled. Air was entering her chest through her wound. She needed to be moved now. Satomi looked up to see Audra atop the back of the perpetrator and no one else available to help her move Ryder.

"Keep putting pressure on it. I'm going to get you out of here."

Ryder gave a small half smile, although it wrinkled through the wet tears. She gasped to gain air. Satomi didn't want to pull on Ryder's shoulders and interfere with the pressure Ryder was placing on the wound. She had to act fast. As Ryder grew weaker, her ability to hold pressure would lessen as well.

She grabbed Ryder by the ankles and told her to hang on. Satomi had never noticed how uneven the ground was or how many rocks were scattered about, but now she did as Ryder's head bounced up and down. Ryder groaned with each jostle. This was the best Satomi could do. Everyone was busy.

They finally made it into the office, where Mary and Jia waited. Satomi would talk to them about needing the courage to go into the midst of battle when the time was right, but for now she was worried about this injury. They helped her place Ryder on the cold metal table. Satomi cut Ryder's shirt to reveal the wound.

She didn't need to use a stethoscope on her friend's back to know what was happening. Her breathing was distressed and, away from the battlefield, she could see one side of her chest did not rise. She wiped blood from the wound and placed a plastic wrapper over it. She directed Jia to hold it tight, but to pull it away from the wound occasionally so pressure wouldn't build. Mary worked to establish an IV. Meanwhile, Satomi prepared the Lidocaine and necessary tubes.

"Ryder, your lung has collapsed. I have to place a chest tube."

Ryder nodded, not comfortable enough to speak. She would lose consciousness soon.

Satomi located the fourth and fifth ribs. She prepped the site and injected some Lidocaine. She'd need the rest for the deeper layers, which would only get more painful to the pleural, the potential space between the lungs and the chest wall that was no longer potential. She worked as quickly as the local anesthetic would allow. She didn't want to put Ryder into further distress. They had no oxygen tanks to supplement her and she also did not need her moving. Jia and Mary stole glances at the wound in silent horror as they performed their tasks.

Satomi probed with her finger to ensure she was in the

proper location, making cooing noises to comfort her pained friend. She placed the tube, sutured it in place, then inserted the other end of the tube into a two-jar system she pulled from the cabinet. She watched the liquid inside the jars bubble as air came out of Ryder's chest cavity, unable to return to put pressure on the lung.

"They wanted medical scientists. They wanted you," muttered Ryder in between faints.

"It's OK. I'm here. I'm taking care of you. You're going to be fine," said the confident Satomi as she turned her attention to the offending wound, but guilt racked her. Should she have gone out there sooner? Her vow - had it allowed harm to come to Ryder?

Mary had gotten an IV in place. They both assisted her in cleaning and stitching the stab wound. With the worst of it over, Satomi gave Ryder another dose of their valuable pain medication to help her sleep. Ryder needed to sleep and heal.

Satomi treated the superficial wounds that crowded her office. Three men with defensive wounds. One with a sprained ankle. But her mind stayed focused on the frightening and intriguing manifestation of the infection. Those that attacked them had characteristics of both infected and non-infected. Had their experimenters somehow reduced the viral load of the infection, allowing some but not all of the brain structures that had gone dormant to spark and work? A sort of medical brainwashing?

She required that every patient be picked up by a non-combatant citizen and be watched for signs of infection. They waited on stretchers and chairs for their keepers. Was the attack today only physical or was it also biological? They had to take precautions. Satomi called for everyone who'd fought to come and be examined by her.

Temperatures taken. Eyes examined for dilation. Satomi considered a quarantine but knew she didn't have enough evidence to remove freedoms. That was harm too.

Dwyn stuck his head into the office. Satomi took a moment to wipe her brow and sweep back her hair.

"Satomi, we have someone for you to see."

$$*\quad*\quad*$$

"He needs to be in the medical office. He needs to be treated!" argued Satomi. They could set up a quarantine area in the medical office. The laboratory was no place to treat a patient.

She looked into the conference room through the window at the simple brown tarp on the floor, and a man writhing on top of it. The conference table on which Gordon and their first few subjects had been secured had long since been requisitioned for dining purposes. This man's torso twisted and rocked. His arms were tied and his mouth was taped shut. His legs were unsecured, but lay in odd directions. Broken.

"Audra said to bring him here. You're not supposed to treat him. Just examine him. See what you can learn about our enemy," Dwyn tried to explain.

Enemy? That thought hadn't even crossed her mind. This man had injuries. He had an underlying illness. He needed to be quarantined to prevent an outbreak. *Enemy* had nothing to do with it.

"I'm treating him," she said as a statement. There was nothing to argue. She couldn't physically move him to the medical office, but that wouldn't stop her from providing treatment.

Dwyn shook his head, giving up, and left. She imagined he'd go get Audra to set her right. She'd set *Audra* right.

Satomi entered the room and closed the door behind her. The white walls held one white board whose markers had long ago dried out. Along the walls were stacked papers - white papers, lab reports, and journal articles from the previous staff and a previous life. Satomi approached her patient. He was built strong with wide shoulders and no muscle atrophy. His brown curly hair wrapped around his face and met his also-curly beard. He was covered in blood - his or others, Satomi had to determine. Underneath, his blue-gray skin had elasticity to it. His eyes were sleepy.

His legs would need to be set. He had a gash in his abdomen. Probably the inciting injury that had led to his fall and broken legs. It would be stitched.

"What have you learned?" asked Audra entering the room.

"Both of his legs are broken. They will need to be set. Superficial wounds to the stomach. I'll wash those out and close them. Shouldn't be a problem."

"Shouldn't be a *problem?* This is a *big* problem, Satomi. I need to know what's going on here. What is this?" she gestured to what she considered a creature in their building.

"It's a patient."

"It's not."

Satomi would continue her exam and hopefully also get Audra's information as well. She searched for an entry point for the infection. He kicked at her with broken extremities. Scars were scattered across his body, but there was no fresh bite.

Audra stood in the corner, arms crossed, and exasperated. She had changed shirts, but she was still matted in blood.

Satomi pulled on the eyelids and revealed dilated eyes

with a cloudy gray. Inside his mouth, his teeth were decaying. Satomi untied his shoes and pulled them off to reveal a decent stench and sores. It seemed he had been wearing those shoes and remnants of socks for days, weeks maybe. Potato sack tunic uniforms suggested a system in place.

The sickness was specific and the numbers revealed purpose, not accidents. Human survivor, z-virus, death - these were all distinct states at one point, but this specimen and what she had seen from her window, brought that all crumbling down. They had a permanent supply of these soldiers at their disposal. They created and took care of their army systematically, not haphazardly.

Audra didn't want her to treat him. Ryder's words rang in her ears. They wanted her. Why did they resort to fighting if they just wanted medical care?

CHAPTER SEVEN
SCOUTING

Audra stood near the mess hall atop the two-foot tall fountain wall with the bloodied fence as her backdrop. The bodies had been cleared, but crimson stained the broken concrete and gravel. The hidden families hadn't stayed hidden for long. Their timid heads poked out of windows and doorways. Women and men ushered the handful of children back into their rooms before flooding Audra with questions.

"We were attacked today," explained Audra. "The leaders called themselves Jack and Jill. They commanded zombies like I've never seen. They seemed half infected. They appeared to take commands, could climb fences and use knives, and they required a brain injury or excessive blood loss to die.

"I don't think this was their entire army. This was an

expendable number meant to test and scare us. Which seems, based on your actions, you submit?"

She eyed the thirty or so who stared at their feet, kicking some of the blood-stained gravel around. To ask them to fight was a lot, but she didn't have anyone else.

"What choice do we have?" asked Ziv, his bushy beard flouncing around even after he asked his question. Audra noticed that Ziv had been conveniently missing these last couple of hours. Unsurprising. He had a history of cowardice, but Audra had seen him try. Disappointing today. Several nodded in agreement with him to add to her frustration.

"We don't have to sit here and wait for their next move. We can make our own. They haven't gone far. I recommend a scout group follow and find out what we are up against. Maybe we can figure out a weakness, or what they want, maybe even take out their leaders. We can become more trouble than we're worth. They'll move on. Would anyone be willing to join me?"

Audra realized that if they weren't willing to defend their homes, they probably weren't willing to venture outside of them. She waited in the shameful silence.

"You should stay here," said Dwyn. "This place needs its leader. It doesn't need you gone on a scouting trip."

Not only did no one volunteer, but Dwyn didn't even want her to go.

"I'm not your leader," she said, but even as she said it, she knew it wasn't true. She didn't see anyone else standing up. She knew the council and Ryder had wanted her leading even before all this. "Ryder is."

Noises of confusion and disagreement erupted. "Where *is* Ryder?"

Satomi gave a report. She was stable, but still had a road to recovery.

"Until Ryder is better, you're the leader," called out Tranter, who was here with his cured wife. Everyone nodded in agreement. Until then, it was all Audra. Audra accepted it, but she wasn't going to sit cozy while others scouted.

"Look, I'd love to stay," she lied, "but I've the most experience tracking zombies. And that's what we're going to be doing - tracking zombies. I have to go."

"I'll go too, then," said Dwyn. If he couldn't keep her here, apparently, he'd tag along.

"And I," called out Gordon.

"Not this time. You stay here," she replied to Gordon. She didn't want to leave Osprey Point defenseless if something went wrong. Gordon was surprised by this, but nodded.

"I will go," said Satomi, a quiet but clear voice. She stood resolutely with her hands behind her back.

"Don't you need to care for Ryder?" Audra questioned.

"No, yes, I mean, she's stable. She's going to be OK. I'll have Jia and Mary care for her for a few days. And she *won't* be OK if we don't figure this out. They wanted scientists, doctors, I heard. You need me to come so we can figure out WHY, what they want exactly."

She was right.

"What about your other patient?" Audra asked sarcastically.

"He is stable, stitched, and if we can keep him off his legs, they should heal properly."

"Have you tried the antidote on him?"

"Wait!" yelled out Tranter. "You have one of *those* here?"

"Yes, he's our prisoner," replied Audra calmly. She was not about to listen to their opinion on prisoners if they weren't going to be a part of any defense.

"The cure?" she asked again.

"No. I want him to heal before we do that."

Audra wasn't surprised. She needed answers and Satomi wanted a patient. She needed Satomi on her side, though. When they returned, she'd argue her point again. For now, she let it go.

"Ziv?" Audra asked for his company.

"Really? Do you need me?" His face contorted. His bushy eyebrows pressed together in concern. He pulled at his beard while he waited for an answer.

"Yes, I need your scientific expertise to help us figure out what we're up against." Audra didn't want him here, hiding.

"You're up against maniacs," he proposed.

She also didn't want him here, spreading lies and rumors to justify his fears.

"Maybe. That's why you're coming with. You'll help us understand." Audra wasn't going to take 'no' for an answer.

Ziv seemed to understand and conceded. Audra wasn't outright disagreeing with him. He would go along.

Thankfully, no one wanted to argue about the keeping of the prisoner, and they had their scouting group formed. Audra stepped down from the fountain, signaling they were dismissed. The men and women left to tend to their children and watch for signs of infection in those who had fought.

Audra and the others disappeared to gather their belongings, which were no longer neatly packed every morning, but daringly left out in their rooms with the promise that they would be back that same evening. It was a weird feeling, and now it was over. Audra knew they wouldn't be the only ones packing at Osprey Point.

Everyone would be getting ready to bolt, packing their bug-out bags just in case Audra's crew came back with bad news or didn't come back at all.

Audra didn't blame them.

*　　*　　*

With the group packed, they trekked to where Audra had found the first half zom, then continued down one of Audra's forest trails. The dirt was soft and dry, and showed the traffic that had come through.

Once again, Ziv had packed too much. She watched him juggle his bag from left to right shoulder in attempts to stay comfortable. Satomi overtook him with her slim bag. Audra gave Ziv a small pat on his shoulder but did not stay for the complaint as she also passed him. As she did, she caught the metal scent of blood still on her. She had washed up, but certain movements still kicked up the scent and with her senses in overdrive, she noticed each time.

She pulled up alongside Satomi and touched her elbow. Satomi gave a weak smile with her bottom lip. The corners of her top lip were carried up rather than smiling themselves. In the women's last few interactions, Satomi had been a pain in Audra's backside, but she knew she had good intentions. She was glad and concerned Satomi had volunteered to come.

"Lay it on me, Satomi. Are you coming to seek revenge?"

"No... I can't as a doctor."

"Um, yes. You can." Audra didn't see what her profession had to do with her motives and actions. In fact, she could think of plenty of ways a doctor could get revenge.

"You see. I took an oath. 'First, do no harm'. I take it seriously. It's my mission statement, I guess."

Audra's eyebrows rose in doubt. "You can't just not do any harm. How do you protect the ones you love?" She thought of Ryder. Surely, Satomi would harm for her.

"I protect my loved ones by taking care of them, not by killing."

Audra wasn't sure if Satomi's mission statement could hold up. *Someone* had to fight to make things better. She had fought an army just an hour ago. Jack and Jill needed to be cut down. Larange Greenly needed to be cut down. *That* was how they protected their loved ones.

"Then why are you coming?"

"Their need for science work and medical care is going to be their undoing. It will be important for us to know."

At least they agreed on one thing.

Jack and Jill did seem to want something specific. Audra imagined they didn't need much of what else their small community had, but medical care and scientists were hard to come by.

Audra noticed the shuffling footprints had veered off the road, and pulled left away from Satomi. The zoms had gone off the path. Broken branches and kicked-up leaf litter met Audra's keen eyes. They either hadn't been taught or hadn't been commanded to hide their tracks. The others fell in behind her, trying to weed their way through the leafless woody plants that tangled and pulled.

Audra's heel was clipped a couple of times, but not by vines. Dwyn was tight on her heels, following like an overenthusiastic puppy. He asked her tons of questions about tracking - half of which she swore she had taught him before. Audra imagined he was happy to have a chance to talk to her. At least it wasn't romantic advances.

"Do you think Jack and Jill are a couple?"

Or, maybe it was.

"Why, do you want to date her or him?" shrugged off Audra, pretending she was focused on a particular muddy smudge.

"No... no... I don't think so. I just wondered. They seem to be some sort of pair." He paused behind her to check out what was so special about the smudge.

"They're at least a Jack & Jill."

"A who?" he asked, leaping to catch up to her.

Audra shook her head. She wasn't going to explain.

She heard a grunt from behind her. It sounded like a zom. She turned her head. No, it was just Ziv. At the back of the pack, trailing along, and of course, grumbling.

"Why don't you come up here as a mating call?" she called out over her shoulder.

"What?"

Audra shook her head. She wasn't going to explain.

In fact, she shouldn't have said either of those things. The snark was overflowing without much filter. And she knew why. Because she had failed them. And she'd rather point out their weaknesses than sit with her own.

Audra had known they were out there. Not Jack and Jill specifically, but that evil, wicked groups could march through and destroy everything they loved. She should have prepared them more. They were so focused on a cure, they had forgotten the uninfected could be the real problem now.

A small hand touched her shoulder. It was Satomi's. She didn't say anything. Audra appreciated the gesture, but felt crowded with the two, Dwyn and Satomi, on her heels.

"I'm going to run on ahead. Just a bit. Get a head start on this trail."

Audra was anxious to see what lay at the end of it.

There had to be a reason they had gone off the easy track. Perhaps just the direct route. What did they care about some cuts and scrapes?

"I'll go with you," said the ever-present Dwyn.

"No, you stay here with these two. Practice the tracking I've taught you so far to track me. I won't be far. I'll double back if things get wacky."

She looked ahead where the sun glittered and the wind danced through the trees. She scanned the roots uncovered by low-clearance feet. And with that she kicked the two off her backside and wandered deeper into the woods.

Alone.

Where she belonged.

CHAPTER EIGHT
THE CONVOY

Audra continued to track the zombies through the woods, but she realized they were nearing I-16, the highway which emptied into Savannah. Audra had run miles and miles on these grounds, but hadn't realized they could be such a straight-shot from the highway. It wasn't exactly a marked exit.

She kept a steady pace, giving Dwyn markers to follow until she saw light from the clearing ahead. She attempted to pause at the forest line that delineated the highway, but found the line had blurred since she had last come through. The forest had crept and crawled onto the roads. Cars in the median had been swallowed up with weeds. Only vehicles firmly on the expressway were not being attacked by greenery. That wouldn't be the case in a few more years' time.

On the nearest side of the highway, the two lanes of cars had been cleared out of the way, haphazardly, but cleared nonetheless. Like a parting of the rusted sedan sea, the cars in both lanes angled outward as if someone had driven through the middle. Some were just pushed to the side, while others had wheels and axles broken. Glass and plastic scattered the cracked asphalt where weeds shot through and flourished. Audra dared to get behind a sedan and peeked her head down the line. The parting was far, but she could see something a mile or two down the road, something that was now taking up the middle spot. A convoy of sorts.

Jack and Jill had told the truth. They were not local. They were traveling, and thus, hopefully, not many in number. Numbers settled, made homes, farmed; small groups traveled, camped, and scavenged. Here their enemies were set up on I-16. Audra eyed the ragged forest line and the broken cars strewn in the ditches. There was plenty of cover for her to reach them and spy on their operations.

Audra turned and headed back to her scouting group. She shouldn't run off without them. If they found the highway, they might not be discreet in following the convoy. They'd need to do it together. At least this was something to give them, after her failure hours ago. She had found their resting spot. They'd figure out how to stop them and Jack and Jill would die and rot on I-16, just like everything else, until the brush consumed them.

*   *   *

Audra was now happy to have the crew on her heels. She needed them to be nearby and quiet. Ziv pulled up close to her. He kept yanking on his beard nervously. Satomi and Dwyn walked in a pair behind him. Only the odd zombie in otherwise abandoned cars took notice of them. The zoms slammed up against gray smears on the windows, leaving further marks, their eyes dark and sometimes a yellow piece of plastic flashing from their ear. Tags. Tags from a bygone era when Audra thought that Lysent cared for the sick and would come scoop them up as soon as the cure became more abundant. How naive she had been.

Audra noticed Jack and Jill hadn't scooped them up either. Did they convert zombies into soldiers or did they start with healthy humans? The latter thought made Audra feel sick - which in turn, washed her with guilt. They were *all* humans. Their zombie status shouldn't make something more or less sad. It was all sad and it had to be stopped. Still, Audra feared for her comrades. Could they be recruited into the zombie army?

As the team got close to the convoy, they dived deeper into the forest. They did not want to be seen approaching, observing, or leaving. The journey was slow in the brush and everyone seemed to be deep in thought, worried about what they might soon find. When they reached the tail-end of the convoy, Audra signaled for Ziv and Satomi to fall back deeper into the forest. She and Dwyn would investigate first.

An RV marked the end of a line of over ten vehicles. RVs, passenger vans, eighteen wheelers. The fuel needed to move such things had long deteriorated in their region. Where had they found a reliable fuel source? Beyond the RV was a horse trailer. Arms stuck out and rested on the low bars. Eyes peered through dark shadows without a word - half zoms. It was hard to reconcile such human-like positions content in a trailer. The two held back gasps as they reached some sort of modified eighteen wheelers.

The simple metal sheeting of the trailers had been replaced with transparent heavy acrylic. Within were many stalls, two stalls high. Holes for air flow lined the top and bottom, reminding Audra of the visitation room at Lysent. In each stall stood a person. Some wielded knives, some bows and arrows, some grenades. They were like toy soldiers packaged for any specific need. Through the stalls, Audra could make out a sort of hallway that allowed entry and egress. Then, another layer of stacked zoms. Many more than what had attacked Osprey Point.

Audra imagined the redesigned vehicles weren't highly durable, but they didn't need to be. Visible even from here, metal protruded from either side of the first truck in line, some kind of plow. They cleared vehicles off the road and these trailers followed.

A cleared highway with full access might have been convenient long ago, but now it was dangerous. Audra remembered being doored last time she was on this highway. Nothing good could come from it, just more enemies. The cars were worthless. Trunks had been pilfered of their blankets and snacks long ago. If Audra never had to sleep in a back seat of a musty car again, it would be too soon. She preferred almost anything makeshift in the woods over laying her head on rotting cushions.

"Where are they heading?" whispered Dwyn.

Audra shook her head. She didn't know. Wherever they wanted, she guessed, but it did seem to be a big production to just wander.

"Do you see anyone? Any place for medical care?" asked Dwyn.

Audra didn't see anything. They just seemed to be transport.

While they saw many, many zoms, they didn't see many

humans. In fact, no humans yet. Dinner maybe? Audra counted the vehicles - there had to be at least that many drivers. Fifteen vehicles - five transparent trailers, a couple plain trailers, the truck, a couple of cars, the horse trailer, and several passenger vans. Depending on what was in the plain trailers, could be thirty humans, could be much more. Did it matter? Even if they could separate humans from zoms, thirty would be too many to handle.

Audra stopped calculating the number of zombies when she saw something moving in between the trailers. She ducked farther into the ditch. A man weaved in and out among the trailers. His dark hair moved side to side on his head as he looked around. He seemed to be on the lookout, but not for them. With a look behind him, he crept past the vehicles and headed toward the woods. Toward Audra and Dwyn.

There wasn't much time to react. The two started backtracking out of the ditch and back into the woods. Hopefully he just wanted to do some illicit task out of sight. Audra didn't intend to stay and find out. They quietly fell back, slipping into the brush. The man was being quiet too, until he whispered.

"Hey, don't leave. Help me." Audra and Dwyn looked to each other. Why was he seeking help outside the group? Maybe it wasn't his group. "Please. They're going to turn me into... one of them."

Audra felt sick with the thought. The man crouched, searching for them. Why didn't he just run? Audra would be running, but then again, she was a runner.

"Please?" he whispered again as he walked blindly into the woods.

"Hey, I'm Dwyn!" Dwyn said as he stepped out. Of course he did. Without any discussion or even an apologetic look, he was out in the open. Audra shook her head. He was still as naive as when she'd first met him, and she still didn't believe it.

"Hey, hey, help me. Those crazy people fed me, helped me, but they're just fattening me up... like for the slaughter, but worse. They've got these crazy crawlers. They're like-"

"We've seen them," cut off Audra as she stepped out too. She glared at Dwyn, who was unscathed by it. Audra glared harder, but it did no good but trigger a sheepish grin and a shrug.

The man was just a kid, maybe late teens. His dark hair frazzled in waves over his fair skin. To his benefit, he did look scared or maybe his eyes were always that buggy. Bright blue. Green flecks.

"Where did they find you? How many are there? How do they convert them?" spouted off Audra.

"Whoa, dude, I'll tell you everything. You just gotta get me out of here first," he said, looking behind him once more.

"Of course," said Dwyn, approaching the kid and putting his arm around him. "Come on, we've got some supplies. Hungry at all?" Dwyn began to lead him to Satomi and Ziv. "What's your name?"

"Dennis."

There was no way in hell Dennis was coming back with them, but he could have just the information they needed. Audra allowed and followed behind them, one hand on her knife.

They found Ziv and Satomi sitting on a rotting log. They stood up and let Dennis sit down. Dwyn pulled out a food bar from his bag and offered it. Audra was not as impressed. She stood, watching out for any outside noise, with one eye on Dennis.

Dennis munched the oat bar. His eyes darted around

as if the group might change their mind and take it back. He did seem hungry. It was easy to forget how hard life could still be. Osprey Point could be crowded and boring, but at least there was food and shelter.

"Cool beard, man," he said to Ziv, his mouth half full.

Ziv nodded but didn't say anything in return.

"Dennis," redirected Audra, "this group threatened us with those... things. Do you know anything about them?"

"They're some sort of smart crawler. Jill told me that they found them like this. That these people were in the process of getting better. That's why they are more human than crawler.

"But, I get the feeling that they're... creating them. I mean, I've never seen anything like them in the woods or in the city. Have you guys?"

Audra shook her head. The half zoms were definitely being created, maybe by some bastard version of an antidote.

"I started thinking." Audra thought that was probably a strenuous task for the guy. "I started thinking, 'why do they have me around?' It's not like we were picking up every Sue and Sally. They were just feeding me. Not asking me to do any work, although I pitched in to help. I was pretty skinny when they found me." Audra thought he was skinny now. "Then I decided they were trying to get me healthy before they made me into one of *them*. Why else keep me around?"

The half zoms were strong because they transformed strong humans.

"Do they feed the zoms?"

"What? Yeah. Disgusting job. I kept throwing up, so they dismissed me from that task." So, raw, maybe still live flesh. "And there's more..." Dennis hesitated.

Audra and the others looked at him expectantly.

Instead of speaking, he swallowed the last of the oat bar with the slowness of someone who might not be fed again. He carefully moved his hand to his jacket. Audra responded with her blade.

"No, no, it's not like that." He moved even more slowly and pulled open his jacket to reveal a bright red spot on his shirt, stuck to his side.

"I feel fine for now," he assured the group. "I think it takes time to transition. I'm sorry I didn't tell you earlier. I just can't stay with that group. You wanted to know why I thought they wanted to transform me? It's because they did, or will, or have. I don't know. I don't know what will happen after this bite. But word is - you've got a cure? Do you think you can cure me?"

Audra put her knife back into its sheath, but did not let her hand go far. His eyes looked desperate. This was an infected man. Once he turned, he'd chase them tirelessly and attack them violently. At least that's what was *supposed* to happen. Audra admitted things had gotten weird lately.

"What bit you? A real zom or one of those half ones?" she asked.

"Half ones? What? No, this was a full-fledged crawler. But it must be the first part of my transition, right? I don't want to turn into one of them, any of them. You've got a doctor, right? Maybe he can fix me."

"I'm not a 'he', but I'll try my best," said Satomi beside him.

"It's *you*? You came out *here*?"

"Yes, can I see your wound?" She put her hand on his shoulder.

Audra's head tilted in concern. She interrupted the doctor's impromptu physical.

"Let me pat him down first."

"Is that OK?" Dwyn asked for permission.

Dennis nodded as Audra had already begun her search. He winced when she ran her hands along his ribcage that housed the infectious bite. No weapons, not even a knife. Still, she wouldn't underestimate him. He had survived this long somehow.

Audra gave a nod to Satomi to proceed, but remained close to their capture, rescue, whatever he was. Satomi had pulled out her first aid kit and lifted his shirt, and began dressing the wound.

"Have you always been a doctor?" he asked in an attempt to distract himself from the pain as she cleaned the wound with antiseptic.

"You mean before? No, I was too young before. I learned from a doctor. He tried to give me a broad education, not just stuff I would always see, but also stuff I might not. I think he wanted to impart the large knowledge base he received in medical school. He didn't want acupuncture or radiation treatments to disappear. Of course, I didn't have acupuncture needles to practice with. We used knitting needles in a man made of hay. I learned about chemotherapy, but don't have the supplies or even a way to detect cancer. I was a scientist too - gene therapy, biochem," she shared as she worked, mostly just to help distract him. Satomi was a good doctor.

Dennis pulled down his shirt and thanked her. He licked the crumbs off his lip.

"Do you - you think I can come back with y'all?" he asked. "If you give me one of your cures, I can work for y'all. I'm a hard worker."

"Of cour-" started Satomi, but Audra interrupted.

"I don't know about that."

It was one thing to give him an oat bar and some gauze in the woods. It was quite another to bring someone from

Jack's and Jill's camp into their community.

"He can't come back with us," said Ziv, finally making his voice known.

"We can't leave him here!" cried out Satomi.

"What's the difference between curing a stranger and curing Dennis?" asked Dwyn.

"Cause Jack and Jill will be looking for Dennis, that's why," retorted Ziv.

Dennis looked furtively from one person to the other as they argued about his fate. Audra watched him. It worried her that she sided with Ziv. Wasn't he the one who had selfishly hidden? But as much as she hated to consider it - Dennis was a liability.

"Why are we even discussing this? He needs the antiviral and we have it. End of story." Satomi began packing her things to leave as if the matter was settled.

Audra considered the options as the others continued to argue. Leave Dennis here, he'd change, Jack and Jill would find him and add him to their collection. They'd be facing one more half zom. Take him with them and risk pissing off an enemy that outnumbered them. Audra didn't realize they were surrounded until it was too late.

Ten half zoms closed in with knives drawn, forming a circle. Their scouting group had been too loud or Dennis had been a trap. Audra looked to Dennis. He began to cower. Perhaps he hadn't known. Audra shook her head in anger - angry with herself for letting them get ambushed. They had stayed too long arguing.

"Dennis dear," said a syrupy voice weaving between the men. Jill emerged, a head shorter than her soldiers, and swept her blond plait off her shoulder. "Who patched you up?"

Dennis stared at the ground and mumbled, but did not give up the name of his physician. With the snap of her fingers, the circle grew smaller.

"It was me," said Satomi stepping forward and looking Jill in the eye.

Jill pointed and Satomi was grabbed by two half zoms. Audra advanced, but two others moved into her path. Their large knives were held to attack.

"Anyone else educated here?" Jill asked.

Ziv. Ziv was a scientist, but no one gave up that information. And Ziv did not offer it as freely as Satomi had.

"Release her," Audra commanded. She tried not to let her voice waver. She pretended she had any say in the matter, that she had something of consequence behind her demand. She did not. She was wildly outnumbered.

Jill pretended to think about Audra's request for just a moment.

"...No. You will get her back when we are done with her. You had your chance to negotiate peacefully with us. Now we're just going to take what we need."

And with that, the zoms raised their blades at the remaining three. Audra went to move forward again, despite the threat. A hand grabbed her arm and held so tightly that she knew she would see bruises in the shape of Dwyn's fingers on her arm before the day was through. She could free herself, but the vice grip reminded her. There was nothing to free herself to, just death by blades or teeth. She was nothing, on the losing side. She bit her lip until it bled coppery juices into her mouth. She glared the daggers she wished she could unleash into Jill's body.

"LEAVE!" demanded Jill with an authority in her voice that Audra could only wish for. Audra spat shiny blood from her mouth. The metallic taste diminishing. She felt a dribble on her lip. With a snap of Jill's fingers, her crew holding Satomi and Dennis fell back toward the highway.

Audra had walked away before. She had left her sister in Lysent's hands, but now anger boiled to her very rim. Audra was going to get Satomi back. She would not lose another to a vicious bully.

She would not.

CHAPTER NINE
CAPTURED

A thousand thoughts flashed through Satomi's mind as she was ushered out of the forest. Dennis. Was that a trick? No, the current fear in his eyes was real. The infected were directing his movements as much as hers. He needed treatment or he'd turn soon. Ryder. Someone would need to take out her chest tube in a couple of days. Would she be back in time? A jab in the back of her ribs to move her along discouraged that thought.

Dark smoke began to waft through the air - vinyl, rubber, plastic, and something salty-sweet. The doctor in Satomi winced at the fumes, followed by her stomach. It smelled awful. Satomi could feel her lungs gathering goop. What was the point of creating such poor conditions? The small fireball was now visible, a car up near the front. A circle of people gathered near. Gruff men walked alongside gruffer sick.

At the top of the circle stood two matching green and white striped lawn chairs. Jack, she presumed, sat in one and Jill took her spot next to him. Satomi was placed in the middle of the circle. Dennis was on his knees, whimpering and talking to himself.

"She's a doctor AND a scientist. How did we ever get so lucky?" asked Jill of Jack.

"I know a few things," lied Satomi.

"You know more than a few. We saw you in action. You were the one that pulled the leader into the medical office. And sounds like you're the one who treated Dennis," said Jack.

"I'm sorry I tried to run," cut in Dennis.

A laugh. "Didn't you think all of us gone was a bit convenient?" Jack suggested.

A setup. For her?

"'Fess up," Jill said turning back to her. "You came because you wanted to get a closer look at our... creations." She had a smile on her face, but it did not extend to her eyes. She flicked her long blond braid.

"They are presenting with some peculiar symptoms. Would you like me to treat them?" asked Satomi, impressing herself with her audacity.

The entire circle of people burst into laughter. Even the car seemed to spark a little more in response. The green paint melted and peeled along the edges. Thick billows of blackness escaped the broken windows and all the seams.

"No... we don't want you to treat them. They are quite excellent the way they are."

"So, you did it on purpose?"

"*On purpose* would be a little inaccurate."

"Were you trying to cure them?"

"Call it a byproduct. We did. Now we call them soldiers. You'll be making more of them. I guess we need your help, less as a doctor - more as a scientist."

Satomi said nothing. More than a doctor, she was a scientist. And they wanted her to make more of these sick people?

"But for now, please show our guest - uh, what's your name?"

"Satomi."

Jack and Jill and the rest of them looked at her with judgmental eyes. She imagined that they were considering her name hard to pronounce. Satomi didn't offer a shortened version, Americanized version, or a nickname. She didn't care what these fools called her.

"What?" she challenged.

"Nothing. Just the name of our last doctor. You all seem to be Chinese."

Satomi wasn't Chinese.

"What happened to the last doctor?"

"She stopped helping us," Jill said simply as she waved her hand and two guards came to Satomi's sides.

Satomi wasn't sure if another doctor was a scare tactic. Why would they get rid of a doctor if they didn't have a replacement yet? Then, the thought occurred to her that maybe they were getting rid of the first "Satomi" now. As if on cue, something made a bump noise. She looked to the car, where smashed to one of the few remaining windows was an infected and burning woman. Her black hair had incorporated into her face. Jack and Jill laughed at both of the women.

Satomi shuddered involuntarily as she was escorted away. *It's just a scare tactic. It's just a scare tactic.* She repeated to herself. Still they killed - or more accurately - didn't kill that woman to get to her. It was clear that they had not made the same vows she had. It was amazing that she could keep her cool with a scalpel in her hand, but now she trembled with each step away from Jack and Jill.

Her captors.

She was in trouble.

Her escort led Satomi to an old police car being pulled by a truck. She could make out that at one point it had read Wade County. To protect and to serve. She was put in the back, where there were no interior door handles and the seats were made of hard plastic. The windows had been replaced with rebar spikes. The door slammed with a distantly familiar sound.

A car door shutting, heard from the inside. It had been years since she had heard that sound. It was an odd thing to consider in her dangerous situation.

The escort stood over the car, a large, round man. Before she settled, he slipped her a water bottle through the rebar.

"Thank you."

"It's all you get today," he grunted before he stood a distance off and watched her with menacing eyes. Satomi figured she should be thankful that he wasn't trying to trade favors with her.

Maybe that would come later.

The replaced windows brought some air exchange into the car, but not enough and most of it smelled foully of burning vehicles. Satomi was glad it wasn't sticky hot, but she might be chilly tonight. Thick plastic separated her from the front of the car. The floor too was made of the hard plastic. Easy cleaning. No comfort. She curled up in one of the bucket-forms of the hard plastic. Waves of shivers came over her as her body suffered in her stress.

Where were the others? Were they trying to get her back? Audra hadn't wanted her to treat Dennis. She could tell. If she hadn't, maybe they wouldn't have been ambushed. Maybe she wouldn't have been captured. But wasn't their entire community built around giving the cure freely? Audra might be OK picking and choosing, but Satomi always extended her oath to the entirety of the universe, and that meant treating everyone placed in her path. She hoped she could continue that here.

A wave of tiredness crashed into her. A lot had happened and there was much more to come. She should rest if she could. But every time she closed her eyes she saw that woman, cooking, in that car. She imagined she could smell her, even now, over the burning tires. She hoped that she was dead by now, but in her heart, she knew she wasn't and at the same time, it felt like she was wishing herself dead.

CHAPTER TEN
AFTERMATH

Dark poisonous smoke filled the air and followed Audra, Ziv, and Dwyn back through the woods. It was all coming together. Jack and Jill were the ones who had set the fire yesterday. What did they care about visibility? They had an army of foot soldiers and cannon fodder to do their bidding. And now they had Satomi.

The march back was painfully slow. Ziv couldn't keep up with a run. And as much as Audra wanted to dash off to Osprey Point and fix this, she also could not leave the last two of her crew alone. No one else was disappearing under her watch. So instead of a run, they walked. Quietness roared, interrupted only by the crunches of brambles underneath their feet. Ziv, for once, didn't complain. Audra would've lost it if he had. She should have gone alone or at least should have stopped Satomi.

"We shouldn't have treated that Dennis piece of sh-" she muttered, half to herself. She kicked at a root before stepping over it.

"It's what we do. It's what Satomi does," Dwyn replied.

"Well we shouldn't. He probably agreed to that bite."

"Satomi wasn't wrong to help. No one would agree to being bitten. Pain takes over and you're trapped. You're trapped in your own body with no place to go. I'd never let anyone go through that if I could stop it. I can't tolerate seeing anyone in that state. I can feel it."

"You can feel it?" she asked, stopping and turning to look him in the eye.

"Well, not really," he backpedaled.

He hadn't said it directly, but Audra had heard it. She could hear the pain in his voice. It seeped through his words and imbued them with another layer of meaning. He *remembered* how it felt.

"You've been infected?" and before he could answer, "You knew about the pain."

Dwyn's eyes shifted, avoiding her gaze.

"I only knew of *my* pain. It wasn't until Gordon that I was able to confirm my experience. I didn't tell you, because I didn't want you barreling into Lysent and getting yourself killed." He was always trying to protect her. "And then, and then, I just didn't know how. I didn't think it mattered."

Didn't matter? Belinda had suffered for years because Audra couldn't let her go. If Dwyn had been a zombie, then someone had cured him.

"Who?! Who did you know in Lysent?" she rounded on him. He had never offered his connection.

"What? I don't know anyone at Lysent." Dwyn looked confused.

Ziv awkwardly shifted from one foot to the other.

"Well then you knew someone rich, who was she?" As soon as Audra said it, it was clear to her. It was a she. Vesna? Vesna didn't have the courage to tell her that she had just spent all her money curing this dimwit?

There was a stale pause in the air.

"Corette. Her name was Corette," Dwyn offered in a soft voice. "She was my fiancée. We got caught up by a couple biters. Early on. I tried to hold them off. A year or so ago, she cured me."

Jealousy, pain, and shame swirled in Audra. This Corette had succeeded where she had failed. But if she had cured Dwyn, why weren't they together?

"Where is she?"

"She's married to some rich guy. He gifted her a cure. She felt guilty I was infected and she wasn't. They pulled me out of the car she had left me in and I was cured a few days later."

"Must be nice." Audra's voice dripped with disgust. Cures as gifts.

Ziv pulled on some bark of a tree.

"Yes, it was, eventually... I woke up and thought everything was going to be the same. Nothing was the same. She wanted nothing to do with me. I had all the feelings I had for her then, but she had moved on in the time I had lost.

I was alone and cashless. I needed to find a way to survive quick. Vesna helped me, saved me again really. And then you were the best thing to enter my life, there in the woods."

There. That push. Over and over.

"Are you serious?!" she reeled on him. "You're constantly on *me* to share my feelings and to share my bed, and you don't bother to tell me you were infected!

You say you want me to lead our group but then you constantly push me out of the way or hold me back. 'Best things' require trust."

Dwyn's clinging was just the outcome of his sob story. Everyone had one and now she knew his. The front of her head burned with anger, but her eyes stung with tears. She jerked her head back ahead and stomped onward. The two men followed wordlessly.

CHAPTER ELEVEN
BYPRODUCTS

A honeyed "Comfy?" invaded the vehicular enclosure. There weren't many women in the convoy.

Jill.

Satomi uncurled and separated her skin from the plastic divots. She refused to stretch in Jill's sight or comment on her accommodations. Instead, she sat up in one of the bucket seats and looked over to her as if they were passing on the highway. Her terror had transformed to numbness and she'd pass it off for confidence if she could.

Jill worked the handle and the car door creaked open. Satomi climbed out wordlessly but did give a look of curiosity. Was she about to find out what Jack and Jill wanted of a scientist? The sun was just starting to streak brightly at its fresh angle. It highlighted the dew on the reflective markers and the ambitious weeds that sprouted from the asphalt. Jill headed farther up the convoy, meaning for Satomi to follow. Last night's guard followed the pair. Vehicle after vehicle, until they reached their destination. An eighteen-wheel trailer with large graffitied metal doors. Maybe some ancient gangs. Satomi remembered a different world where people would smudge "Wash me" in the grime.

The guard managed the heavy latch, then Jill took one side and the guard took the other. The large metal doors were pulled open to reveal a mobile, scavenged laboratory. One wall was lined with large machines - refrigerators, freezers, a sterile hood, and digital ovens. The other side contained counters with rows of smaller equipment, microscopes, hot plates, a fancy centrifuge and an array of beakers and flasks on racks and stacked test tubes. Satomi had seen nothing like it as a mobile setup. The back had anchored tables with miscellaneous equipment and stacks of books and notebooks.

They seemed to have everything they needed except for staff. And Satomi guessed she was it. She tried not to show delight in her new prison. She at least stopped herself from climbing in without a word of instruction.

"The soldier serum is given to those infected with the z-virus. From there, their motor control and coordination improve. So does their ability to receive commands.

Dr. Bren developed the serum, but eventually she refused to keep making it for us."

"The woman in the car?" Satomi interrupted.

Jill gave a stern and satisfying nod. Satomi felt torn. Dr. Bren had created a horrible weapon, but then she'd had a change of heart? She stood her ground and was killed over it.

"So you can't make any more 'soldiers'?"

"Not right now. That's your job."

"How am I supposed to do that? I don't know the first thing about the soldier serum." All the equipment in the world didn't matter if she didn't have any foundational knowledge of the serum.

"Dr. Bren's notes will be available to you. In seven days, we will test your first batch and mark your progress."

"Human experiments?" Satomi squeaked. She hadn't even considered being here a week - or beyond. Suddenly life felt both long and sweeping by.

"I encourage you to get up to speed and make progress quickly. I also encourage you to accomplish the goal if you don't want to be replaced." Jill crossed her arms and nodded toward the entrance.

Satomi's guard gave her a hand up before heaving his body up the height as well. Jill laughed as she closed the large doors behind them, leaving Satomi at the laboratory's edge under the guard's watchful eye.

Away from Jill's coarse demeanor, Satomi let out a sigh. She felt her shoulders relax and she could breathe. She looked around the trailer. Large sun windows and strategic flood lights illuminated the space. She'd never imagined a laboratory with all its possibilities would be a prison. It was at least better than the cop car, and the scientific equipment elicited a certain peace. They intended these tools to destroy, but she could use them for good.

Satomi walked along the counter and fingered the small tools at her disposal. She turned to the man with a dark mane and a rare potbelly. It was the first time they were alone and isolated, but he didn't cast any dark shadows her way. She gave a small smile.

"I'm sorry. What's your name?" She was tired of her only anchor being nameless.

"Eli," he said. He stood with legs wide and arms behind his back at the trailer end as if she had anywhere to escape.

"Hi Eli. I'm Satomi. Will you tell me more about this serum I'm supposed to make?" She leaned against the counter, hoping to glean as much information as she could.

"What do you need to know?" His stance did not change, but he seemed willing to answer a few questions.

"Why did Dr. Bren develop it?"

"To protect her people."

"Why did she stop?"

"She changed." His voice faltered. He glanced downward.

"What do you mean?"

He straightened up to compose himself. "How is this supposed to help you make the serum?" he asked with his chin up.

"I'm not going to make the serum," she confessed. "I practice 'First, do no harm'."

"I don't know what that is, but if you don't make the serum, you're going to die like she did," said Eli. He didn't say it like a threat, just as if it was a matter of fact.

"I guess, I am," resigned Satomi. She opened the fridge to see what was inside.

Familiarizing herself with the lab, last touched by Dr. Bren, felt like her last rites.

"Where are Dr. Bren's notes?" she asked, looking around.

She could at least learn as much as she could about the soldier serum and how it interacted with the z-virus. Maybe even how to reverse it.

Eli pointed to the back of the room, where a work table with stacks of papers threatened to fall over.

Notebooks of various age scattered the surface with notes hanging from all their edges. A disarray of information.

Of course.

"Why the car?" she asked out of her morbid curiosity as she walked gingerly over to the mess as if it might attack her.

"They burn the cars anyway. It smells awful. But Peter likes it."

"Who's Peter?"

"Their dad."

That was beyond disturbing, but she had learned something else. Jack and Jill were siblings. Next, she'd sort through some of these papers.

*　*　*

Sleep slipped away against the scraping reverberating through the plastic. It took more than a moment to remember where she was. Not in her soft bed pad, not in Ryder's room, not even at her desk having drifted off during late-night research. She was in a police car, captured by a group with an army of the sick. She wasn't allowed to sleep in the laboratory. 'It's only for working,' they said.

Satomi rose softly, trying not to alert Eli. A lantern bobbed, illuminating one man dragging another along the road - the source of the scraping noise. So many men here. The rest of the convoy was dark. Everyone had gone to bed.

"What's wrong with him?" she wondered under her breath.

"Sick. Has to be disposed of," said Eli, not missing a beat. He must have heard her stir.

"Can I help?" she said at volume. 'Sick' had many

meanings here. Which one was this?

The man towing the sick stopped. Both he and Eli peered into her dark vehicle to see if she was serious.

"I'm here because you want more of *them*, right? Wouldn't treating this one keep your count high?"

The man on the road dropped his keep. "Get out," he said as he approached her abode. His blue-black hair was pulled back into a ponytail. As he got closer, Satomi could see he was darkened red by the sun and alcohol. Flecks of spit and other items ran through his beard. Satomi's stomach dropped. She backed away to the other side of the car.

"No, wait. Why?" she asked.

The door swung and bounced on its hinges. A large hand groped into the darkness of the interior and found her. She clawed at the smooth plastic but found no hold. He ripped her from the car and threw her on the ground at Eli's still feet. The asphalt felt cold and wet-smooth. Satomi pulled herself half up to look at her abuser.

"You want to help? Let's go then." He pulled her to her feet by her shirt collar. It cut into her neck, and the seams made popping noises but held.

Satomi found her feet, slipping at first, and his arm moved from shirt to arm. Eli fell in line behind them. He grabbed the sick man by the wrists and dragged him along. His body sounded heavy and thick with the ground's moisture.

Satomi tried not to think about where she might be going or the heavy hand on her arm. Instead, she focused on the reflective white dashes flashing in the light of the man's lantern. Tears pooled in her eyes and slipped into a stream down her cheeks, but she remained calm. She wished Eli was on her side. She could only hope she hadn't suggested leaving the safety of the car for... she didn't know.

Satomi looked up to see the lantern light reflecting oddly off of clouded eyes inside the acrylic cubicles. They remained passive in their captivity, not seeking the edges of their enclosures to reach them. Strong men built wide and no attempt to escape. At Osprey Point, Satomi had restrained the infected prior to recovery, but this was different. This was simply humans in cages. Satomi diverted her eyes. She focused on the highway markers again.

They passed the trailers. When they reached a plain container van, the man let go of her. Satomi smiled through her tears at the 'WASH ME' scribbled in the dust of the side panel, despite herself. The man disappeared in front of the van and Satomi dared to exhale since they appeared to have reached their destination, and it hadn't ended with her being pushed into the van - yet. He returned with a rolling stretcher of dark blue vinyl and metallic chrome, most assuredly taken from an ambulance at some point. Satomi disapproved. He hadn't bothered to use it for transport earlier, instead choosing to drag the sick by its arms. The two men heaved the sick onto the stretcher.

She heard his labored breathing and something within her clicked into action. She was here to help. While she still feared for herself, whatever happened afterward was not her concern at the moment. She walked assuredly to her patient and immediately saw the problem. His shin swelled and showed a red color that his gray could only sheen over. An infection.

"What happened to his leg?" she asked. She touched his forehead, forgetting she did not know a normal temperature.

"He cut it. We cleaned it up and stitched it up, but it's

infected."

"It's more than infected. Something's in there. It'll have to be removed and the infectious material cleared before he has a chance."

"Don't tell us what needs to be done. Do it," said the man. He opened the back of the van to reveal an array of medical supplies. Satomi's eyes brushed over the inventory as the light allowed. At first glance, they had an abundance, but she realized amounts were sporadic and disproportionate to priority - the result of scavenging. How much would they be willing to part with?

She grabbed a blade, forceps, four by four gauze, a stitching kit, and a bottle of Betadine.

"Do you have any anesthetic?" she asked, looking over their shelves.

"They don't feel pain," the man said, arms crossed tightly.

Her patient's grimace said otherwise.

"The shock could kill him," Satomi tried.

"We don't waste anesthetic on the dead." He was unmoved.

The dead? Satomi rounded on the guard.

"HE'S NOT DEAD! If he was dead then having a doctor would be worthless!"

The man was not fazed. "Whatever. Either do something about it or don't."

Satomi looked back at the 'dead.'" They saw a disposable soldier. She saw sickness covering grief, pain, and confusion. She would help. Of course, she would help.

"These instruments need to be sterilized," she said as she set them down with the lantern on the foldout table Eli had positioned by the stretcher.

"They're clean," said the dark-haired man with a tone

that said he didn't care, not that he knew.

Satomi shook her head and grunted her disapproval.

He added, "Do you see a hospital around here? This will have to do."

Eli had not contributed to either side of the argument.

"It doesn't *have to do*. At least get me a flame. We'll sterilize that way."

It was his turn to make noises of disagreement.

"Start another car fire for all I care," said Satomi. The woman flashed involuntarily in her mind's eye. "I'm not introducing more bacteria into this leg. While you do that, I'll prep the leg. Do you have any narcotics?"

"Not for the dead."

Satomi shook her head and began to prep the leg. The light was barely sufficient. It seemed the deep woods soaked it up. No narcotics. No anesthesia.

It was going to be a long night.

CHAPTER TWELVE
NEW LIGHT

Audra had wanted to arrive at Osprey Point as quickly as possible, but with the cloistered community in her sight she hesitated. She had promised answers and instead she had lost their doctor and her friend. She had awakened them, brought them here, and now she was failing them. Would they stay and help her or would they scatter like cockroaches in the light of their new enemy?

They slid the gate just barely so Audra and her team could slip in, no longer generous with the opening into their community. The metal sheeting had been rinsed but small tufts of hair clung onto the edging. Dried blood had turned rusty brown in little crevices. Little indents marked the metal. The gate had seen battle.

Audra wasn't sure what system of communication had been put in place, but they seemed to assemble as soon as she stepped inside. No chance to put off what she didn't want to share. She walked up to the defunct fountain. A thin pyramid made up the height of the statue, atop which was a large ring and a swooping bird. For the first time, Audra realized that the eagle-looking bird with the impressive wingspan was probably an osprey. The empty pool underneath had muddy concrete and brass metal nozzles protruding from its surface. Audra sat on the smooth tan-orange limestone wall, tired from their fighting, scouting, and retreating.

A woman in a long ponytail offered her some water, but Audra waved her off. Yes, she did need food and water, but she would wait. This was more important.

"Where's Satomi? What happened?" asked Jia, the woman from the medical office. She pulled at her curls in worry. They straightened then sprang back up.

"We came across a man asking for help. He ended up being bait for an ambush. They took Satomi."

"Well, maybe they'll leave us alone now," suggested Tranter. "That's what they wanted, right?" The skin around his eyes wrinkled.

There were some nods of agreement from the crowd and only a few looks of concern. Audra balked. These saved survivors were so ready to give up on one another.

Audra stood up. She pulled her tired body onto the limestone wall to make her point. "I won't leave anyone to those people, least of all, Satomi. We need her here and she needs us."

"Maybe we can contact Lysent," said another, standing near the mess hall. "Make a deal with them and get under their protection."

Several more nods filled the community. Most of these survivors hadn't had personal experience with Lysent.

"Let's not get carried away," suggested Audra, who

was ready to toss them all out on their asses. "Lysent kept the cure from you. They'd have you still wandering the woods to be captured by this Jack and Jill for their army. None of them care about your survival."

"And you do?" asked Tranter. "Honestly, I think your personal grudge against Greenly is keeping us from good food and security." Tranter was apparently the voice of bubbling dissent. He leaned against the laboratory front as if he was part of the assembled leadership.

"If you think I need to step down, I'm all damn for it. I don't want to lead a group that hides while their leader fights, and abandons the doctor that cares for their every need.

"Get the F out of here if you only care about your own skin. Trade your first born to Lysent or enlist as a half zom. Why should I -"

Audra felt Dwyn's hand on her arm. Tranter had struck a nerve. They were outnumbered, outgunned, and she'd just handed the enemy what he wanted. And maybe she did have a grudge. Audra sank at the thought that she did not have Osprey Point's best interest at heart. Didn't she?

She took a deep breath. "Let's just go over our options before we run to Lysent. The cost may be more than we've considered."

Could she swallow her pride and allow Greenly to be her solution to her Jack and Jill problem? Lysent could be the thorn they needed in Jack's and Jill's side.

Audra stepped down from the short wall and let the crowd disperse. She had no answers for them. Her shoulders pulled on her neck into a giant ball of tension in her chest. Audra made her way to the mess hall. She needed food in her belly, then to find her bed before she collapsed in the plaza.

"Audra?" came Ziv's voice.

It was only then she realized Ziv hadn't been the antagonizing voice in the crowd. The fact that he wanted to speak with her privately surprised her, but it didn't make his complaints less tiring. She missed his march back in fearful silence.

"I think we can neutralize the army," he offered quietly.

Immediately Audra was all ears. Hell yes. She looked around to see if anyone was listening. She didn't want their opinions at this point. She knew what they wanted - to run into the arms of anyone who promised safety.

"How? What's your new plan?" she asked, pulling him to the side by the laboratory. Its stucco walls held onto green grime and dirt.

"Actually, it's an old plan. Vesna's plan."

"Aerosolizing the cure? I thought that didn't work."

"We stopped trying when Vesna died. We're more familiar with modifying the cure now.

"I'm sorry, I know I've failed before. Vesna died, your sister died, because I couldn't figure it out."

"It's not your fault, Ziv." She placed a hand on his shoulder.

Ziv stared at the ground, evidently not comforted.

She tried again. "Aerosolizing wasn't the solution then. And the cure wasn't the solution for my sister. Redirects happen. They aren't failures."

Ziv met her eyes. Audra had never spoken to him about her sister's death. "Aerosolizing could be the solution to these half zoms, but what do you think Jack and Jill will do with the people afterwards?"

It was a moot point. Audra would set Lysent on Jack and Jill. Lysent would win, but wouldn't gain anything but a bunch of cured zoms. Ziv's plan was just what she needed.

"We can only give them the opportunity to fight back," she lied. "Can you start on this first thing tomorrow?"

"Sure. It shouldn't take me too long." He rubbed the back of his neck with his hand. "I only have to half-cure them, right?"

Audra leaned against the lab for support as she laughed through her exhaustion. He wandered off, letting her be.

With Ziv working on leveling the playing field, Audra just needed to find a way in, a reason to speak with - and distract - that king and queen pair.

CHAPTER THIRTEEN
EARL GREY

Time scrambled by as Satomi worked and came to a painful and frightening halt when her work was done. During the day, she studied Dr. Bren's notes and pretended to work on the serum. At first, she couldn't make heads or tails of Bren's lab notes, but when she accounted for the idea that these notes did not start post-outbreak, but instead began before, she was able to sort the years of notebooks.

Dr. Bren had worked for Lysent.

Not the Georgia division, but wherever she was from. Lysent was a global company, and to think that their branch was the only one who had been given cures for safekeeping was limited thinking indeed.

There were notes on the virus, modifications for the cure, the soldier serum, and some other serum. The formula for the soldier serum looked straightforward, but Satomi would not be following it. Satomi also couldn't figure out why Dr. Bren, who was possibly involved in the pandemic itself, had decided to stop cooperating and landed herself in that burning car.

Satomi was trying her best to stay out of the car herself. Jack and Jill realized the benefit of keeping their current 'stock' healthy, and the list of untreated injuries was long. She spent her nights treating the soldiers. In between her shifts, she was allowed a couple of hours' rest and a small meal of scavenged or stolen food, Satomi was not sure which.

On the second night, she had received a thin blanket. She was undecided whether it best served as a pillow, a buffer from the plastic, or as a layer of privacy as she rested. She ached. She ached so much. She didn't understand how Audra and the others had survived sleeping away from civilization for so long. Although she imagined that if they chose to sleep in cars, they did so in ones with upholstered seating. She refused to complain. Hostile interactions, bad sleep, and crappy food were on par for medical providers.

Finally, time to walk back to the laboratory. In just a few days, she had learned their routine, route, and the purpose of all but a few vehicles. The one they passed now, she assumed to be Jack's and Jill's residence. In the back, the metal doors had been sealed shut. Instead, a real wooden door, a window, and a stoop had been installed, like on a real house. Today, the curtains in the window fluttered and the door opened.

"Pleasure meeting you out here today!" said an older man as he stumbled on the height of the stairs. He straightened up and smoothed the wrinkles from his tartan shirt. "How are the children?"

He greeted them as if Eli and she were married and they were all old family friends. His haircut and beard were neatly trimmed and his clothes were clean and pressed. He was like a time traveler. Satomi just stared.

Eli left her side and went to usher the man back into the trailer. "Sir, sir, you really need to go back inside. It's probably time for tea. Did you leave the kettle on?"

"The kettle?" He glanced back at his home, but then rounded on Eli. "What's it to you!"

"Nothing to me, Peter. Nothing. I'm sorry," Eli apologized, obviously flustered. So, this was Peter, Jack's and Jill's father... and Eli was trying to keep him from her. Why?

"Hi!" Satomi said brightly, matching the man's greeting.

"Hello, dear..." The man searched her face as if trying to remember her name.

"Satomi. It's nice to meet you, Peter." She came over and her hand rose to shake his. She trusted that Eli would let her advances slide rather than escalate the scene further. Peter shook her hand.

"The tea!" he shouted and without letting go of her hand, he pulled her toward the door. She gave Eli a sly smile and followed in. Eli looked clearly exasperated, but Peter's comfort seemed to be the priority here, and she'd take advantage of it to learn more.

"Come in, come in. I'm sorry to say you're late. I already put the tea away. But no worries, I can bring it out again. Just next time call if you'll be late," he said, backing up so she could get through the doorway.

He continued. "Will your husband be joining us?"

Satomi looked at her gruff guard, who did not advance from the stoop.

"No, I think he has some errands to do."

"Oh ok," he said, but seemed to notice that 'the husband' made no movement to go do said errands.

Satomi smiled. "Can I help you put on the tea?"

That seemed to bring him out of it and he welcomed her farther into the home. Satomi let out a small gasp.

"I know it's a mess! I'm so sorry. I wasn't expecting company," he tittered as he wrung out his hands.

"No, it's pristine. It's so beautiful! What a lovely home!" She felt a pull to keep him happy too, even though she had just met him. But the truth was, it was pristine. The walls and ceiling were done in paneling, highlighted with exposed decorative beams, high windows, and skylights. A sitting area with a loveseat and table for four, a kitchenette, and a partitioned area of a presumed bedroom created a residence with anchored furniture. The whole place was decorated in white and pink roses. Embroidered pieces hung on the walls.

"White and pink. Laura's favorite colors. I don't care for them much, but I can't stand to get rid of them now. It's how I've lived, you know?"

"Of course."

"I wouldn't know what color to do it in. And the paint store is so confusing. I don't even know what my favorite color is. Just that Laura's were pink and white."

"I think it looks wonderful. She did a good job," Satomi whispered as she was led to the stove to help with tea.

Peter's gray hair was thinned, and his skin had the papery characteristic of age, but he moved with confidence and agility.

"Do you get to go to the paint store much?" she ventured.

"What? No! Do you work there? Why are you here?" he turned on her with an angry look. Another episode.

Dementia? Alzheimer's? Satomi remained calm.

"Tea, remember? It's me - Satomi - here to have tea with you. OK?" she asked for permission.

"OK. But don't sell me any encyclopedias."

For a moment Satomi thought it was a continued lapse, but he had a sly grin on his face. It was a joke. At least that one was.

They sat down with their dandelion tea next to a framed photograph that featured a young and happy Jack and Jill. Besides their blond hair, their plaid shirts matched.

"Jack and Jill?" she asked, pointing to the photo.

"No, no - Peter and Evelyn. My babies. That's their senior photo. Inseparable those two are. You'd think they're twins."

She did think they were twins. They looked close in age. And it was both their senior photos?

"They graduated at the same time?"

"Yeah, Peter got held back a year. Although if you ask me, they just wanted to be together. Perfect grades ever since. They're in college now. Learning medical stuff. Doctors, I think. I'm so proud of them."

"I'm sure you are," Satomi whispered.

This pink and white home revealed a softer side to the siblings. After another few minutes, she ventured again.

"Do you know your house is on wheels?"

"I suspected as much. Otherwise there are a lot of earthquakes." He laughed.

Satomi laughed too.

"Do you know where you're going?"

"Everyone moves these days. We're just a-moving."

"Thank you for my tea. Dandelion is my favorite."

"Good for you. Mine is Earl Grey. Not available in the stores nowadays, I guess. Global warming or some shit."

"Something like that," she said. "If I find any Earl Grey, I'll bring it by for you. It's been a pleasure having tea with you. I'm Satomi. What's your name?" she tested him.

"You don't know my name? Why…it's…" his face crinkled. "What's it to you anyway?"

Unable to recall information on command, and anger to hide it, typical of Alzheimer's.

"It's OK," she said. "Thank you for the tea," she repeated.

"It's not OK. Get out of here!" he yelled with a large start, knocking over some silverware and upturning an empty cup. It chipped on the side.

"See what you made me do! Get out!" he yelled again.

Satomi did not need to hear it a third time. She had overstayed her welcome. Before she reached the door, his demeanor had changed again.

"Have you seen my wife?" he asked sweetly. "Please let her know to come back. I just need her to come back. It will all be OK as soon as she does. I just need her to come back." He muttered over and over.

Satomi's eyes watered, not sure if him thinking his wife left him was better or worse than the truth. Eli received her at the stoop.

"Happy?" he asked when the door closed, referring to her escapade.

"Is Jack's real name Peter?"

"Jack is Jack." The man huffed. He either did not know or was not going to tell her.

Eli continued escorting her to the laboratory. Satomi's mind reeled. Satomi was a doctor, and she had just figured out how to benefit Jack and Jill without breaking her oaths.

CHAPTER FOURTEEN
PROPOSALS

The burned-out car broke Satomi's routine on the seventh day as she was brought to the meeting area. The gray and black smoldering of last night's fire pit marked the center and she stood just beside it. Two empty lawn chairs waited under the awning of a recreational vehicle. Before long another circle of men formed.

The man with the ponytail and beard brought in a z-virus patient on a leash and pole. The patient pulled and struggled against the device and all the outside stimulation. Satomi did not have to look hard to recognize the man with the now-ashen face and dark hair as Dennis. Her hand clammed and perspired around the syringe she was to inject him with.

Satomi knew she had taken a big risk not working on the soldier serum for the last four days. She had researched the notes heavily to inspire her newest route, but rabbit hole or not, she had been given orders by her captors and she had not fulfilled them.

And Dennis could die because of it.

She could die because of it.

Satomi stared numbly at the car, even though she knew she shouldn't. All the glass, plastic, and paint had given way. It was patched of black and ash white. If it was a scare tactic, it was a good one. Satomi imagined Ryder arriving to rescue her and being directed to the police car as Eli set it on fire. *Would she ever see Ryder again?*

The recreational vehicle's thin metal door opened with a clatter. Jack and Jill both tried to exit at the same time and fumbled over each other. Jack gave his sister a playful shove and came out first. Jill followed. The crowd laughed and cheered. Jack flounced down into his lawn chair, which creaked with the sudden weight. He flung his leg over the arm rest, which bent wide.

"Are you ready to show us your progress?" he asked.

"Perhaps she should thank us for her accommodations, first, Jack," said Jill, sitting down more gracefully. She played with her fishtail braid as she waited, staring at Satomi intently.

Satomi was hesitant to address them. "Um, yes. Thank you for keeping me safe so far. I appreciate the opportunity to work with the soldiers."

"Treating soldiers is worthless if we never get any more serum," said Jill dismissively, turning her eyes to her braid's end.

Satomi was very clear on their priorities.

"I understand you want to build an army, but I've thought of a better use for your resources and I think you'd agree."

A look of exasperation played on both the siblings'

faces. How were they not twins? Ignoring Satomi's words, Jack tapped his fingers on the closest plastic arm rest.

"Get on with it," Jack said to Eli.

Eli grabbed Satomi roughly, which surprised her. He had never really touched her the entire week they had been together. He yanked the syringe from her hand, then moved toward Dennis, who had been forcibly pinned to the ground with the leash and pole.

"STOP!" Satomi shouted. "I think I can cure your father."

Eli froze with one hand on Dennis and the syringe in the other. He looked to Jack and Jill for direction. Jack raised his hand, and Eli let go and stepped back holding the full syringe.

"How do you know about our father?" asked Jill, arching back to relax into her chair.

"I met him, by accident," she replied, not wanting to get Eli in trouble. "He has some sort of early-onset neurodegenerative disease, right?"

"Uh something like that. What makes you think you can cure him?" asked Jack.

"The soldier serum," Satomi replied as if it explained everything.

"You are NOT going to infect him," said Jack firmly. Jill sat more upright in her chair with her disapproval as well.

"No, no, I'm not. It's just the soldier serum proves that you can modify the virus! You can keep some of the 'good' things about the virus and circumvent what's bad. Dr. Bren designed a serum that modified end-metabolism so that the infected could move better, but kept the end-neurotransmitter levels low so that higher brain functions remained damaged. Willpower and sense of self stayed lost."

"And what would *you* design?" asked Jack.

"The z-virus triggers an excellent cleaning system in the brain, destroying malfunctioning and dying cells. It also bolsters neuroprotective properties. I'd use that to heal your father. But, I'll prevent the virus from consuming neurotransmitters so all high brain functions will remain intact."

"We'd have our father back?"

"If I can make it work, yeah. But, you have to agree to not make any more soldiers."

Jack and Jill looked at each other. Satomi assumed they were doing that sibling non-verbal communication thing to discuss their options. Dennis struggled, but he and the soldier serum were quickly forgotten.

"Deal," said Jack. "What do you need?"

"I need to build a peptide. I have the right equipment, but I need a biopeptide anchor medium."

"All right..." puzzled Jill. "We'll take your word that's a real thing. Where can we get such an... anchor?"

"If anyone can find it, Audra can. She's your best bet."

"Your friend from your compound? She's *your* best bet. Remember what happens if this fails."

Satomi didn't need reminding but glanced at the sedan all the same. She knew what would happen. Death, one way or another. But she knew this was her best bet to keep her oaths, and herself alive. Eli handed her the syringe back, and Satomi pocketed the prepared saline with a hidden smile.

*　*　*

Audra sat munching on greens in the mess hall when the alarm sounded. It felt like confirmation to her nerves, which were already on high alert. She wasn't sure what she expected when she peeked through the reinforced slats on the gate, but her breath caught in her chest when she saw the long black hair of the half zom. It wasn't Satomi, but it *was* purposeful. The zom trudged forward. An arrow with a white flag fletching protruded from her chest. It secured a paper note, sealed in salvaged plastic.

Seeing no other signs of movement in the forest, Audra slipped through the gate and reached for the note. The zom made no motion to stop her. Upon closer inspection, the zom's body bloated and the glassy orbs of her eyes bulged. Audra pulled the note gingerly, avoiding the sticky masses of blood that clung to the wound and plastic.

Jack and Jill wanted an audience.

Audra's heart ached to see Satomi, and each step in their run drew them closer. She was happy that Gordon and Marcos had volunteered to come. She was still upset with Dwyn.

This time they spent no time in the forest line, but instead marched straight into the convoy. Two men escorted them to a central area where some of the vehicles had been circled around a campfire site. Even maniacs needed camaraderie and company, she guessed. The lawn chair thrones that held Jack and Jill were laughable, but Audra lost the thought when Satomi was brought to her. She gave her a giant hug. Her body felt thinner. Audra apologized that she hadn't been able to set her free yet.

"Are you OK?" Audra asked.

"I am. I really am." She exchanged hugs with Marcos and Gordon.

Audra pulled her close again and searched her eyes for the truth. She did, bodily, appear intact. No bruises. She looked tired. Her face was wrinkled in new places.

"How's Ryder?" Satomi asked as another fold climbed her face.

"She's great. We're fighting to keep her in bed."

Satomi giggled. Then, "her chest tube?"

"It stopped bubbling, whatever that means. Should we take it out?"

"Yes, but make sure to perform a Valsalva maneuver when you pull it. Then close it *really* well."

"- a what?"

"Have her hold her breath," Satomi explained.

"OK." Why didn't she just say that?

Jill cleared her throat. Satomi must have taken it as a hint.

"I need a biopeptide anchor."

Gordon nodded. He knew what it was. Audra didn't.

"For Jack and Jill? A what?"

"Yes, sort of. It's a medium used in peptide synthesis." This time the second explanation didn't help. "I wrote it down."

Thank God. Audra pocketed the folded-up paper.

"If you bring us what we need, we will return Satomi after this project," proposed Jack. He sat stiffly on his throne.

"What's it for?" Gordon asked.

"None of your business," replied Jill. Audra and Jill locked eyes. Jill was quickly climbing her hit list, right below Larange Greenly.

Satomi brought her back. "It's OK. Trust me."

It didn't really matter what Jack and Jill wanted in the interim. Audra was playing the long game.

"I'll get it for you." Another hug. "Hang in there, Satomi. I'm sorry you're still in here. I promise to make it right."

Away from the convoy, with the trees wrapped around them, the group breathed a little easier. Satomi was holding up well. She didn't seem abused. They seemed almost reasonable.

"So, what do they want?" asked Audra, confused.

"Satomi wants to make a peptide. Peptides are signals within the body," explained Gordon.

"And what will this one signal?"

"No idea."

He was of little help. Was this going to be used to make more soldiers? To create a new pandemic? The possibilities were endless.

Audra sighed. "OK, you two report back to Osprey Point. I'm going to go scout out this... whatever." She patted the pocket that held the note. She didn't tell the others, but she began getting her bearings for the most efficient route to Lysent from their location. Probably the rail line.

"Actually," started Gordon, "I was going to go out from here." Audra knew what 'out' meant.

"You got a lead?"

"Yes, someone told me a woman and her daughter go by their names in an outpost near Atlanta. It isn't Lysent-sponsored. It's another community. But if you need me here..."

"No, Marcos can get back by himself, right?"

Marcos shook his hair out of his face in agreement.

"She's married," Gordon confessed.

"Well, you guys were divorced, right?" she asked, not sure how that changed things.

"Yeah, yeah, we were." Gordon looked down, interested in the acorn he was pressing into the ground with his shoe. His small glasses fell a bit and he adjusted them.

"I'm sure they'd love to know you're alive. They probably think the worst."

"It *was* the worst," he said, finally looking up at her. "I didn't come home to them when things went south. I was too wrapped up in my work, intent on saving the world, instead of them."

"You did help. Go now."

*　　*　　*

"Well, well, well..." came a voice from the top of the well-manicured gate. Audra knew she wouldn't find tufts of hair on this one. It was taller and the crow's nest was more than a rickety scaffold.

"Hey Charlie," she said, approaching slowly.

"You know I'm supposed to shoot you, right?" He brushed the frizzy brown mop out of his face, but it quickly returned over his eyes. How he could stand watch like that boggled Audra.

"I know." Audra had hoped to have a plan by this point, but no revelation had revealed itself on the run. She settled for straightforward. "I have a proposal for Greenly. She'll benefit from it. I can't help who I am. There is no other way to get in touch... so I uh, came."

Charlie's eyebrows rose at her audacity. "I'll let Lysent know that you'd like to talk to the big boss."

"Thank you. I'll wait here."

"That's probably a good idea. You're not allowed out there, much less in here." He disappeared and another guard took his place immediately. Audra didn't recognize him, but he seemed to accept Charlie's instruction.

Just in case, she walked farther up the road and leaned against a pine tree. With her pack by her side, the bark felt rough against her skin and through her shirt. She rested on its solidness. At least trees were reliable. Everywhere else she was playing a game of fake trust and caution. She pulled a pine straw that stuck into her pants.

Audra dozed for a few minutes, not realizing how exhausted she was until she had settled into the pine straw. An hour passed and Audra was sure that Greenly had decided to completely ignore her request. But then sure enough, the gate opened and two of Greenly's henchmen waited to escort her in. Audra stood up and brushed off the things that stuck to her. A thought settled inside her - if she walked through those gates, there was a chance she'd never walk out again. Greenly could have her head. She took a deep sighing breath, pulled on her pack, and approached the gate.

With one hand by her waist and the other on the strap of her bag, Audra walked inside.

The town hadn't changed much. That didn't surprise her. Investments went into Lysent headquarters foremost, trickled into the township, then to the townships farther down the road. The trickle was... insignificant. Audra hadn't changed much either. She used to bring in tagged zombies here, trying to strike a deal for her sister.

Another deal.

Another sister.

Audra's escorts were two burly men who looked like they ate well. Must be a good gig in Lysent. They stopped her in the plaza outside Lysent's front building. Its tall windows glimmered with extravagance. Before Audra could wonder if it would take another hour to see progress, beady eyes emerged from the interior of the Lysent building. Her salt and pepper hair was pulled too tight into a bun. Her giant guards and her choice of all-black attire made her lithe body appear even more delicate. She walked with confidence and small steps down the white granite steps.

"I'm surprised. Quite surprised. You know I could have you hanged in the next few minutes?"

"I'm aware of that. You're also aware that I hate you. So between those two things, you know I'm here for a very important matter."

Greenly blinked slowly and tried to hide a smile. Audra swallowed hard and spoke before she could change her mind.

"There's a group with a formidable army that has entered our area."

"Is that so? How does that affect me?"

A motion caught Audra's eye. She looked over at the fountain. A bunch of dancing cherubs. Theirs worked. Water flitted from one arch to another. Audra turned back to Greenly.

"It's a big army. A hundred or so at least – well-built, strong zoms and people. I can take out their main strength, but it's still too large a group for us to handle. You have the numbers."

Greenly stared at her, her eyes darkening.

"We can't handle them without you?" she asked.

"If you could, I wouldn't be putting myself and others at risk. They're going to want *your* resources. And as much as I hate you - it's the devil I know. I know nothing about these strangers. I don't want them here and neither will you."

"And what do you need from me?"

"I need this biopeptide anchor thing that they want. That's how I'm going to get in and plant our sabotage. Then you'll come and sweep up the pieces."

Like Audra, Greenly didn't really seem to care what the biopeptide anchor was actually for. She didn't ask. They all had their own games to play. Greenly thought on it for a moment before adding her condition. "In return, I want your corral. Now."

"You're already getting all of the spoils of war," Audra countered. "Why do you want them?"

Greenly knew about her corral? Of course, she did. Maybe not for certain, but they had done the math. Somewhere, Audra had a backlog.

"Hm, more so, I *don't* want them. You don't seem to understand the strain you're putting on the area. And the safety risk." Greenly's arms crossed. One set of fingers gently tapped across her thin upper arm.

Could Audra give up the corral for Satomi? She wasn't really in a position to bargain. She needed Lysent's help.

Audra didn't think hard on it. It was a deal she was willing to make.

With the small insulated box housing the item Satomi requested in her jacket pocket, Audra was escorted by the men through the township back to the gate. Audra heard whispers from people who recognized her. She ignored their murmuring. At the gate, two men sat on horses waiting.

Shepherds.

"Hop on," said one, a man with red hair and a matching grizzled beard. He nodded toward the back of his saddle.

"Can't we run, instead?"

"Hell no. This is the deal. Do we need to talk things out with Greenly again?"

No, she didn't. Audra sized up her two escorts. She didn't recognize either of them. The redhead wore a cowboy hat and sat on a big, black mare. The other, a spindly guy with long, stringy blond hair sat on a smaller spotted horse. Audra looked up to see if Charlie was still on his perch. Maybe he could tell her if these guys were all right or not. Charlie was nowhere to be seen. The guards must have switched out.

Audra breathed a deep sigh. With one hand on her knife at her waist, she offered her other to the man. His giant, rough one swallowed hers and she was swung up into the saddle. Their hips connected. Audra's face wrinkled. He smelled of damp clothes and tobacco.

If Greenly wanted her dead, she would have done it herself, but that didn't mean that she wasn't in danger. The gates opened, and they headed down the road. Before the township was out of sight Audra felt the horse's momentum shift. Her nose filled with his scent and her breasts pressed against his back as she fell into the rider. Audra heard a laugh. He had done it on purpose.

Audra felt the knife's handle in her hand. She imagined digging it into his neck until arteries burst. She imagined him falling to the ground and his dead body being struck by the horse's hoofs as she left him behind. Instead, she just tried to lean back as much as she dared for fear of falling off.

She pulled a red hair from her. Her stomach boiled and threatened to heave over, but she held it down. No need to piss him off. The jostling of the horse didn't help. Audra wasn't used to traveling in a way that didn't use her feet. Her perspective made huge bouncing shifts while her stomach undulated in a lagging pattern.

Audra hadn't had much interaction with the shepherds. As a tagger, she had tagged individual zombies. Shepherds dealt with herds. Audra hoped she wouldn't be recognized for this trip. She and Dwyn had killed two shepherds - Lars and Lindon - who had been sent to move a herd through the laboratory. If things started going wrong, she could run into the thick woods where the horses couldn't go. That is, if she could get away.

Another jostle. Audra's face smashed into his shoulder, but she managed to arch her back away from him. He got nothing that time. The man readjusted in his seat, smashing between her legs. She heard a snicker.

Audra imagined slitting his throat and riding with his body until they reached a place she could string him up. He'd swing in the air like a toy.

"I don't get it, Manny," said the man on the other horse.

"What's that?"

"I don't get how this little girl got Lars. That man was honkin' huge."

They *did* know who she was and what she had done. Audra wasn't sure what that would mean for her, but in the moment, she felt a sense of accomplishment out of it.

Yeah, I took two of yours.

"That's a good point, Blue. I mean... Lindon, I get. Overconfident prick. Course, Lars wasn't the smartest."

Blue laughed. "He *was* a dumb SOB."

Manny laughed too.

Audra hated to, but pointed to a single-track off the road. They needed to go that way. Manny and she took the lead. Blue followed.

Manny let out a low gruff growl that only she could hear. "You can't do shepherds like that. You better watch yourself."

Audra glanced behind her to make sure Blue was still a distance away and not at her back. These two hadn't harmed her yet because Greenly wanted the location of the corral. Audra did not think her protection would extend far after that. Sure, she hadn't told Greenly where the army was located, but it wouldn't be that hard to figure out without her. She was in trouble.

She motioned to another trail, which Manny followed, but not without unnecessarily disturbing the horse to shift her again. After what felt like a lifetime, and not nearly long enough if this was the end of her life, they reached a clearing. Audra pointed to the rusty trailer needlessly.

"Shit, we never thought to look in there," said Manny.

As they approached, the zoms inside smelled the sweaty horses and sweaty people. They riled, grunted, and groaned.

"There's an opening at the top. We drop them in," explained Audra.

"Well, I'll be..." said Manny.

When they reached the trailer, Manny dismounted on the side Blue and his horse were on. Manny held the reins of the horse and looked at her expectantly.

Audra gave him a quick look before jumping off on the other side of the horse. She sprinted to the edge of the field. When she reached the cover of bushes and pine trees, she turned to check the shepherds. Neither of them had given chase. Manny was pulling something out of the saddlebags. Molotov cocktails. He climbed to the top of the metal trailer, lit them, and dropped them in.

The screams were primal. Audra dropped to her knees. The sounds of banging metal reverberated in her ears as the infected tried to escape their hell. Audra hadn't known them to know external pain, but being burned alive was too much for even their pain-numbed systems.

Tears poured from her eyes. Audra didn't care anymore that she might be in the two shepherds' reach. She deserved to die. She had collected all these people with the intent to save them. Instead, she had pooled them together for mass murder. How could she pretend she was doing good?

Sparks and smoke flew from the top of the trap. After what seemed an eternity, when the screams were still not quenched, the two men mounted their horses and turned them away from the wreckage. They were satisfied with the progress. They kept a good clearance from Audra as they entered the forest line again, but it didn't stop Manny from calling out.

"We'll get you. You can't get our own without paying the price."

Audra did not respond, but as soon as they were out of sight, she collapsed into a pool of regret.

This wasn't worth Satomi's life. This wasn't worth it.

*　　*　　*

"Can you really do what you say you can?" asked Eli from the door as she pored over more tomes inside the laboratory trailer.

Satomi wasn't sure if the question was triggered by skepticism or an honest concern for her wellbeing. She didn't look up to figure it out.

"No one's done it before, but the z-virus has laid all the groundwork, I'm just... modifying it."

She turned another coffee-stained page. Dr. Bren had never considered the potential expansions of her serum breakthrough. She had settled for mindless soldiers.

Eli wasn't satisfied. "I don't get it. How can you use the z-virus - something bad - for something good? There's good stuff in the virus?"

Eli was no longer by the door. Instead, he was looking over her shoulder, trying to glean clues from the notebooks she had open. He really was curious.

"The virus itself doesn't contain the 'good stuff'. It replicates inside us until it's consumed plenty of neurotransmitters, then it sends out peptide signals to boost the brain's natural defenses and repair functions. That's why the infected keep going, despite all their damage and the violence against them. If the brain and body live longer, so does the virus."

"Peptides? That's what you were talking about with Jack and Jill."

"Yes, I want to synthesize a peptide. They're just chains of amino acids... simply. It's difficult, but I can do it with the right starting supplies. I'll build the peptide that says to the z-virus that the attack is complete - the virus will skip ahead to the neuroprotective processes that we want for Peter."

"You trick the virus into thinking it's done the bad things, so it will do the good things?"

"Yes!" she cried out, raising her hands, proud of her friend for making the connection. "And that will be hopefully enough to overcome Peter's illness!"

She realized she had just considered Eli her friend. She turned back to the notebooks in silence, but with a shy smile on her face. As much as she trusted him, she knew she shouldn't. He had manhandled her when they met with Jack and Jill. Maybe he had just done it for show, but it scared her.

"Hey... I have a gift for you," he said suddenly. Satomi wasn't sure if he just remembered or if he had just mustered the courage to mention it. She turned on her stool to him out of curiosity. A gift? Better than a favor, she supposed.

"Well, I guess sort of a gift for you..." he said as he pulled two little paper satchels out of his pocket. "Earl Grey, for Peter."

"You heard us?"

"Uh, yeah, it's a trailer. I wasn't going to let you in there and not be able to hear what's going on."

"Oh." Satomi wasn't sure what to make of him.

His eyes watered as he continued to hold them out. And Satomi finally realized it was an apology.

"Thank you," she said. She smiled. He grinned back. "Would you like to go have tea with Peter?"

He pulled out one more satchel. "Yes!"

This time Satomi grinned. She began putting up some of the things she was working on.

"Where are you from, Eli?"

Eli shrugged. "From nowhere, really. Was a bit of a wanderer before wandering was the norm."

Satomi nodded as if she understood. She was reminded again of how traditionally she still lived, even in this world.

"Jack and Jill took me in. Feed me good." He smiled over his belly. "Guess it's better than wandering."

Satomi placed a small bookmark in the notebook and put it on the sorted shelf of books. Questions she had yet to answer still swam in her brain. If Dr. Bren had an inventory of antivirals, then why was there so much research on them and attempts to change the formula? Why had Dr. Bren refused to keep working? In the end, it didn't matter much. She'd use what research she needed and leave the rest. And she'd leave here. But what about Eli? They walked together to the trailer's doors.

"Where I'm from, we can use guards too, y'know... And you wouldn't have to care for hostages," she ventured. She didn't mean for it to be an accusation, but she saw Eli turn his head to avoid her anyway.

"I'm sorry," he whispered as he opened the door and let Satomi step out into the cool air.

"Earl Grey! My favorite!" called out Peter, wrapping Satomi in a hug. He smelled of sandalwood. Satomi glanced at Eli, who was happy to let her take the credit. They were both ushered to the table set with pink and white china. Eli struggled to get his girth into the chair, which was anchored a fixed distance from the table. He smiled all the same.

Peter wore a neat gray cardigan, penny loafers, and pressed slacks. However, his hair was uncombed. He turned on the water before sitting down with them. He happily chattered and rambled.

"Still not sure what color to paint the walls."

"Oh, I still like the pink," said Satomi, happy to see him happy. He was such a gentle soul. She nodded when appropriate. Most of his stories didn't make sense. Satomi poured them tea and Peter was delighted all over again by the Earl Grey. He seemed to be bouncing back and forth mentally a lot today. Satomi worried, but she couldn't make much progress without that medium.

Halfway through tea, Peter started to whimper then cry about how lonely he was. He said he couldn't remember the last time anyone had visited. Satomi was sure that Jack and Jill visited him multiple times a day, but that wasn't true for Peter in that moment. He sat in the chair, overwhelmed in his isolation.

Satomi patted his hand, but he pulled away. She might not be able to help him now, but she *could* help him. She'd create that biopeptide and put his brain into super-powered repair. He might not be completely cured, but he might be able to regain some function.

She just needed time.

Peter could not be comforted, try as they might. Eventually Eli led her out, her heart broken. Their Earl Grey tea sat cold and forgotten.

CHAPTER FIFTEEN
MASS CURE

It was long after the shepherds had left before Audra pulled herself off the ground. She couldn't find the energy within herself to run. Her legs and heart were heavy. Instead, she trudged through the forest. Sharp wisps of smoke spun around the trees, reminding her of the current death. Manny's scent clung to her front.

The adrenaline in her body fell cold and faded into regret. Once again, she dreaded going back to Osprey Point. If only she had the time and money to seek out an old moonshiner, she'd lose herself until penance had taken its course and her liver.

She took whatever solace the woods could provide, and came upon Osprey Point's fences before she was ready. She ignored any greetings she received from above as they opened the gate for her, but one message did catch her ear.

"You're needed in the medical office."

God, what had happened now?

Another whiff of Manny on her chest. Sickness rushed over her. She pushed it down with a loud utterance. Dropping her backpack right there, she ripped off her long-sleeve shirt. She threw it onto her pack and stomped off in her undershirt. It was the guards' turns to ignore.

She walked into the medical office. All the partitions between the stretchers had been set aside. Ryder lay on the farthest stretcher, but no one was rushing over to her. She seemed fine, distracted by the two men near the closet. The top and sides of the closet were sealed with white silk tape.

Ziv and Dwyn looked over to Audra. Ziv beamed. Good news. She needed good news.

"You got what we need, Ziv?" Audra asked.

Ziv grinned as he talked and made large energetic motions. "I think I do! It was difficult, but working from the temperature-stable antiviral actually made things a lot easier. It's just more stable in general. We had only tried to aerosolize that first edition of the cure. We never went back to it after, after -"

Vesna's murder.

"Are you ready to test it on the prisoner? Is the half zom in there?"

"Yeah. Look, I was thinking on it. Is this... ethical? Isn't he like a prisoner of war or something?" asked Ziv.

"Better him first than trying it on all of them, right?" encouraged Audra. She had just murdered an entire trailer of innocent people. She wasn't going to be stopped now by Ziv's cold feet for something that could ultimately be positive.

She could see the gears turning. He finally nodded and

pushed the nozzle of the small tank under the door. Dwyn used another strip of tape to seal around it. Audra heard a click and the faint hiss of gas escaping.

"You look like hell, Audra," were the first words Dwyn chose to speak as they waited over the gassy closet. "Where have you been?"

She'd have to tell them. She didn't have to tell them all of it though.

"I went to Greenly to trade for that bio-pep-thing anchor."

"BY YOURSELF?" Dwyn's hackles rose.

"Yeah, I needed you all here. I used to handle Lysent by myself, all the time," she reminded him.

Dwyn shook his head. "It's different now." He leaned against the wall with arms crossed, pouting.

"How? Cause they don't have my sister to hold over me?"

"No. Because you have a family now."

Audra rolled her eyes. Belinda was family. She had a family then.

"What did you trade?" Dwyn asked.

Audra suddenly felt cold. Goosebumps prickled her arms. The words burned at the top of her chest, hurting to come out, hurting to stay in.

"The corral."

Dwyn slid down the wall into a slump. He didn't look at her, but she could see how wide his eyes were, trying to process it all.

"What corral?" asked Ziv.

Audra put her face into her hands. Rubbed off some of the shame and explained. Dwyn sat in silence. When she told them what the shepherds had done, Dwyn broke down in tears.

"What were you thinking, Audra?" came a voice from

the corner. Audra had forgotten she was there.

"I was thinking that we need to get Satomi back," she turned to justify herself.

"Satomi would never have agreed to this." Ryder shook her head, tears in her eyes. Audra walked over to their disabled leader. The chest tube had been removed and her eyes were clearer - less painkillers at play.

"Satomi won't know. She didn't know we had one in the first place. Doesn't matter what she'd personally agree to. She's a hostage and I'm paying the ransom."

Ryder pulled herself up to sitting with her hands and an involuntary grunt.

"This whole place is built on caring for people. You've effectively allowed mass murder," Ryder accused.

Audra didn't need her to tell her this. She already knew.

After a moment's pause, Ryder choked out, "I'm not sure you belong here."

"What? You're just now figuring this out? Why do you think I don't stay more than eight hours at a time? I might not belong here, but you guys need me. You're not making it through this without some tough decisions and bloody hands. Vesna knew that. Just be happy you can be laid up in bed and hand me the reins."

Audra had never seen that glare from Ryder, usually happy-go-lucky. Her eyes slanted with sharp ends, matching her spiked hair.

Audra turned to Ziv, who waited quietly by the closet.

"Uhm, it will take some time," he said awkwardly about his experiment.

Audra stormed off.

Audra didn't have to be notified of the prisoner's change of status. His yelling from the closet could be heard throughout the plaza. In the meantime, she had retrieved her bag from the center of Osprey Point, washed up, and changed clothes. She returned fresh faced, but still reddened from her tears.

Dwyn and Ziv and one of the nurses, Mary, met her at the closet. Dwyn opened the door, tape peeling on all sides, and they looked inside the three-foot by three-foot pine paneled closet. There the man sat, his splinted legs anchoring him, and his arms flailing. His cries were incoherent, but it was clear he was cognizant and in pain.

Ziv watched in horror of his keep's anguish. Dwyn nudged Ziv into action and they both worked to get him onto the middle patient bed. Mary rushed to give him some painkillers through his IV, which she was thankful was still in place. Audra smiled over their success. These half zoms would be worthless.

"He wasn't ready to be cured. You should have waited for his body to heal," said Ryder. Her face wrinkled in tears.

"No time," said Audra, daring Ryder to argue.

The man whimpered as the narcotics took their course. He'd be OK. This was worth it.

Ryder grimaced and rolled over, no longer facing them. Audra turned back to Ziv. "What's next?"

"I need the trailer dimensions, number of infected, and size and number of exterior holes."

"You got it, Ziv." She turned to leave.

"Audra?" She turned back. "I don't know about the corral. But this - this cure - it's going to be a good thing."

Only because he didn't know the rest of her plan.

Audra nodded.

"I won't let you down," he assured her.

*　　*　　*

Satomi scribbled furiously the protocol she'd follow for the peptide synthesis. She sketched out the portions of the peptide she understood. This work table, mottled with indentations and stains, had become her table.

Eli approached her with caution and sat down next to her.

"What is it, Eli?" she asked. Was it sundown already? She wished she could work on this in perpetuity. The idea was brilliant, but the work was hard. She should have a team. Maybe she could work a deal to recruit Gordon and Ziv. Her mind reeled at the possibilities.

"I'm not sure you should experiment on Peter," he blurted out.

Eli had become a permanent fixture and occasional sounding board in her laboratory. They both really liked Peter. Was he worried about him?

Satomi set her pencil down and looked at him.

"You don't have to worry. I'll make sure the peptide works in vitro first... that is, outside the body. And, if it doesn't work inside Peter and he gets fully infected with the z-virus, then we have a cure."

"It's just, he's not -" started Eli, but he was interrupted by the door opening behind them.

Eli got up from his stool with a creak and scraping against the metal floor. He spoke with the other man in hushed voices. Satomi tried to remember which branch of the peptide she was working on.

"Satomi?" called out Eli.

"Mhhm?" she said, not willing to turn and lose her place quite yet.

"Your friends are here to meet with Jack and Jill."

"Oh!" She turned now, her finger on the spot she was checking. "Do they have the anchor?"

"I don't know, but you'll have to attend the meeting,"

he said.

Eli and Satomi walked to the meeting area, where Satomi was surprised to see the circle of men around the lawn chairs. Weren't Jack and Jill over this intimidation thing? The couple entered and could barely sit comfortably with all the extra armor they had donned. Satomi guessed not. The RV's awning had been pulled back and the sun bore down on the two, casting shadows on their demeanor.

Two familiar faces joined them in the circle. It took Satomi a moment to realize it was Marcos and Audra. It seemed like a lifetime ago, yet suddenly everything she was missing out on came flooding back. Ryder. Osprey Point. Audra did not seem to have any such lapse. Satomi found herself wrapped in a giant hug. It felt foreign.

"Ryder? Did you take the chest tube out?" asked Satomi.

"We did. She's good. Misses you. Are you OK?"

"I am."

Audra pulled her to arm's length again as if to examine her. Audra's face showed worry. *I'm OK, really.*

Marcos gave her a pat on the shoulder. His hand felt warm and heavy.

"Are you sure you're OK?" asked Audra as if seeking a different answer. Wasn't she OK? She pulled her close again. "I'm going to get you out of here," Audra whispered.

Satomi's face buried in Audra's auburn hair. It felt nice. She did feel isolated here, but she had decided her work was important. Something that needed to be done. Osprey Point could wait. Peter needed her here as a scientist.

Satomi heard Jack clear his throat. They didn't like being ignored. She looked to Jill. Jill glared.

"I've got what you've requested," Audra addressed the two. "But I can't give it to you until I understand what it's for." Marcos stood just behind her, arms crossed.

"I'm – " started Satomi, excited to tell her what she had learned, but Jill cut her off.

"I don't think you're in any position to question us." She crossed her legs and flicked her braid off her shoulder.

Satomi and Jack looked at each other with puzzled faces. It seemed Jack also didn't think there was harm in telling Audra what they were doing. It was actually for something good. But he followed his sister's lead and stayed silent.

Satomi looked to Jill. She was tense in her chair, her knuckles turning white against the white arm rests. Her paling lips were tight with determination. She was refusing to show any weakness, and in turn, no humanity. Satomi's heart broke for her.

"I think I am," argued Audra. "I have what you need and I don't fancy giving it to you if you're going to use it to make more soldiers or start another epidemic. We need some accountability here. I won't blindly give this to you when I'm not even going to get Satomi back right away."

Audra was rambling. Why was she rambling?

"You'll get Satomi when the project is finished. This supply is just part of an ongoing trade we have with you," stated Jill.

"A trade? Kidnapping my friend is a *trade*?" Audra rounded.

The trio argued. Why wouldn't they just tell Audra what they were doing here? Why this act? The car caught her eye. Was *that* an act? Satomi wasn't sure what to do, but felt she might be the only one who could prevent this fight.

*   *   *

Audra didn't really care why they wanted the supply. She just needed to buy time.

Dwyn and his four-person team waited off the highway. Dwyn tried to ignore the burrs digging into his arms from their hiding place. He had sent Gordon to scout it out and he reported only five men guarding the half zom trailers. The others must be farther down the convoy or meeting with Audra.

"Glad you're here, Gordon," he thanked the man crouched by his side.

Gordon nodded. "I wish I felt as comfortable approaching my family as I do this army."

Dwyn gave a wry smile. Gordon had made it to the outpost and watched from the woods as his daughter played with her new father. He confided in Dwyn that it felt good to know they were safe, but wanted to wait out this last mission before claiming his own survival.

Dwyn understood. This could easily go south. He pulled a thorn from his elbow.

He could hear Branson and Tess whispering behind him. With Ryder out and Audra and Marcos providing distraction, they'd had to bring rookies out to help. But Dwyn felt they had more than proven themselves when they came out of their homes to fight the half zoms. This was just follow-through.

Behind them, Ziv stood, guarding the tanks they had brought. The green and silver metal cylinders had once carried precious oxygen. Now they carried precious antiviral and propellant. They only had exactly enough, which meant they were probably short, but no one could find another tank in time. Tanks were valuable from the start, and many that had been stolen from their clean environments now lay rusted.

"Tess, come with me. Gordon with Branson. Hit from behind. Disable. Gag. Ziv, stay and keep the tanks safe. Pull out your knife. Have it ready. Everyone got it?" repeated Dwyn.

"What if I need to...?" Branson trailed off.

"Then do, but quietly. I'd love to do this without death, but this has to be done. If they unleash infected on us, a lot more lives will be lost," answered Dwyn.

Dwyn continued with his instructions: "Tess and Branson will work together to secure the exterior air holes and open the doors. As they do that, Ziv will place an antiviral tank and release the gas."

No one acknowledged him, but it was the fourth time he had said it since they had left Osprey Point. Dwyn surveyed the scene ahead of them and held back from repeating himself one more time.

Wooden bat in hand, Dwyn watched the guard turn the corner of the plexiglass trailer, then sprinted after the man with light steps. The flattened weeds from previous traffic presented little noise; so did the asphalt that crumbled to meet the weeds. Dwyn came up from behind and with a hollow pop, the man crumpled.

The half zoms within the cages watched passively. Did they understand what was happening? Dwyn moved to find his next target as Tess bound and gagged the first. He crouched down to check for feet. Far off, he could see two sets dragging a third. Gordon and Branson. He tried not to think about what they'd do next. What he might have to do next. He focused on the next set of feet.

Shit, they were coming toward him.

He rolled underneath the eighteen-wheeler, but it

wasn't much cover. He pulled closer to the shadow. Better, but now he had no access to the man who after passing him would be catching up to Tess, or at least the secured guard. Their cover would be blown.

"Psst."

Dwyn turned his head to the other side of the truck and saw Tess, her blond ponytail swinging down, obscuring her face. She reached out for the bat and Dwyn gladly gave it to her. When the guard passed, Dwyn pulled himself out from under the trailer as quietly as he could.

Not quietly enough.

Dwyn watched the guard's head swivel to look at him, then his eyes went glassy and rolled as a bat plowed into the crown of his head with a sickening crack. The man fell to reveal a sheet-white Tess. Her eyes wide as dinner plates. Dwyn remembered his first kill. He pried the bat from her hands and pulled her into a hug, like Audra had done for him.

"We're doing this to protect our community," he reminded her. Dwyn noticed she had a swath of gray that barely stood out against her white-blond hair.

"Yes," she whispered as she shook her eyes away from the scene she had created. She looked at Dwyn with searching eyes. He hoped she was recalling her children whom she was keeping safe.

"I'll tie him up," Dwyn said gently pulling away, not wanting her to wonder if restraints were needed.

Gordon and Branson ran up to them.

"We got three," Gordon said in hoarse whispers.

They looked down at the mess.

"But not as good as you did," remarked Branson, his blue eyes twinkling.

"Hush," said Dwyn, cutting him off.

They worked together to block the air holes of the

trailers with rags. Tess worked on her belly on top of the trailers to do the top rows. Rag after rag. Pop, pop, pop. It would be Ziv's turn soon. The men inside the plastic boxes did not seem to anticipate any sort of death or emancipation. They stood, all but lifeless, with deadened gray eyes. Their breaths suspensefully slow.

Dwyn looked back and forth, waiting for their enemy to appear and for hell to break loose. What if the meeting broke down and all the men were dismissed? Their team needed to work faster. Pop, pop, pop. He signaled to Ziv. He could start on the first.

Ziv came out carrying two of the refitted oxygen tanks. Branson and Gordon opened the back of the trailer and Dwyn climbed inside, pulling a tank with him. It made a scraping noise. Ziv grimaced and lifted it up higher with regret. He positioned it in the center of the trailer, fully opened the valve, and jumped out. Gordon and Branson closed the doors tight.

One down.
Four to go.

"Look, I didn't calculate for escaped air and the absorption of the rags," began Ziv's usual disclaimers. "I calculated based on complete air blockage from the exterior holes."

Dwyn nodded. It wasn't really time for such discussions.

CHAPTER SIXTEEN
SACRIFICE

Ziv shook his head. An absentminded nod wasn't really what he wanted from Dwyn. He wanted him to realize that applying science to real-life scenarios was tricky and at the end of the day, involved some guessing. What if he had guessed wrong? You have to make assumptions and simplifications. There's a lot to get wrong.

Ziv took a deep breath. He didn't have to cure them all in one go. Any measurable blow would be helpful. He was confident he'd at least get most of them - the ones closest to the pressurized tank. 'Most' was just fine to cripple their army. It didn't have to be perfect.

Perfection was not needed in this instance.

He pulled himself up into the trailer. He didn't realize how tall they'd be, but no one else was asking for help climbing up and down. Tess was on the roof for Pete's sake. He scrambled in, surrounded by strong, ghostly men and women. The transparent walls made him feel surrounded and claustrophobic, even though he knew he was safe. The zoms passed their eyes over him, hardly interested. He set the tank in the center of the trailer. They would be awakened shortly. He twisted the orange plastic valve as wide as it would go and sprinted out as the tank wobbled with the propellant it was not meant to hold. He sprinted then turned around to gingerly climb out. Branson and Dwyn managed to swing the doors fast but then slow them just before they slammed, to keep their actions as quiet as possible.

Three to go.

Branson helped Tess with the last of the rags as Ziv ran back into the woods to grab more tanks. Dwyn followed. He quickly ran past Ziv and grabbed the two, leaving one for Ziv. Ziv's breathing was ragged. His chest burned. He kept telling himself that he'd work out - maybe go for a run with Audra or do push-ups with Gordon - so he'd be more equipped during these missions, but he never managed to bother. His mind was what was needed here. Strength belonged to others.

Great minds seemed to be important in this world, like Satomi's. Ziv wondered what Satomi needed the anchoring medium for as he slung the tank over his shoulder and headed back through the woods. It was obvious she was building a peptide, but what for? Ziv knew Satomi wouldn't create anything explicitly harmful, but she could be manipulated. If she was told it was for something good, she'd do it. She might not even think about how it could be used in a different manner.

He pulled out of his thoughts and looked around for

the next trailer. Why couldn't he stay focused? He could never stay focused. Would he have survived if Jack and Jill had taken him instead? Would he stand and fight? The thoughts haunted him more than he cared to admit. He spotted Dwyn and Gordon and headed toward them.

Another deep breath to try to slow his heart. Lost focus was OK, he just needed to get this done. Perfection was not needed in this instance.

Third tank.
Two to go.

He was doing it. He was out here, helping to get Satomi back. He had feared so often that he'd get here and chicken out. Perfection of willpower was needed in this instance. He felt pulled by all these zoms. He was curing them. He watched them stagger inside their cubicles as the antiviral reached them. They were inhaling their freedom. He did that. Maybe he could be all that Vesna had said.

Fourth tank.
One to go.

Dwyn handed him the last tank, and he and Tess opened the trailer. Ziv climbed in, adjusted the valve and made his way out. He looked to his left and right at the zoms he'd be curing. They weren't looking at him. Their eyes focused behind him. *Why?*

A force smashed into him, throwing his body and momentum out of the truck. They both dove into the ground. Ziv ate dirt and saw out of the corner of his eye that Dwyn and Tess had abandoned the doors to help.

"NO! Close the trailer doors!" he yelled out.

He didn't want the cure to dissipate. He wanted to

make sure the last twenty percent of the army was decimated. He tried to roll over, but a large body was on top of him. He sucked in air and dust as a fist pounded into his back.

Ziv clawed at the asphalt, his nails ripping. He slipped out from under the man's weight and rolled. Ziv noticed the knife flashed in the light despite its lack of sheen. It was an odd thing to consider. He raised his arms in defense. His attacker must have been in there the whole time, had seen the holes getting plugged in. Maybe heard a guard go down. He'd been standing in there with the zoms, waiting for his chance. *Well, he got it*, thought Ziv.

Dwyn and Tess struggled to regain their handle on the doors and get them closed. Ziv heard their slams. They'd done it. He'd done it. Tess held them shut as Dwyn came to his rescue. Ziv hadn't thought to pull out his knife. To him it was a tool, not a weapon. Hadn't Dwyn told him to pull out his knife? The man on top of him had wide eyes and a snarl. Drool fell from the corner of his lips. Ziv yelled out again.

The others - Audra and the others - would hear. It didn't matter now. Their army had been crushed. Just - had she gotten Satomi yet? He wished he knew as the knife found something soft of his. He felt Dwyn arrive, but he also knew it was too late. He felt gutted. But he had accomplished his and Vesna's dream. He'd made it happen.

*　　*　　*

Audra heard a yell, but before she could come to any conclusions, it was closely followed by Dwyn's high-pitched bird call. They had succeeded, somehow, someway. Jack and Jill had heard the yell too and waited for Audra to give them a hint. Now they just had to wait for - BOOM!

That had done it.

"What was that?!" cried out Jill, jumping from her seat, the lawn chair flying back and slamming against the aluminum RV.

"It wasn't us," said Audra honestly, shrugging her shoulders. It was Lysent.

Audra pulled her knife out all the same. She didn't raise it yet. Jack pulled a radio from his belt and asked for a status update.

Nothing.

That was us.

He motioned his men to go check on the armies. "Prepare them."

The man beside Satomi remained. Three against two now. They stared each other down, waiting to learn who had the advantage.

The radio crackled.

We have a situation here.

"What have you done!" Jill screamed out.

She charged at Audra, her ax in hand, her eyes afire and her mouth contorted with fierce anger. Satomi flung herself in between Jill and Audra, arms waving. Jill's momentum brought her and Satomi onto the asphalt. Ashes kicked up in the frenzied attack. Audra wasn't sure how to interfere.

"NOT NOW JILL!" yelled Jack, jumping up.

The pot-bellied man who stood with Satomi launched. Audra was sure it was to assist Jill, but instead his large hands pulled Satomi out of the fray. Satomi went stumbling out.

"You traitor!" screamed Jill as her wedged blade found his leg - high. He doubled over and Satomi scrambled to reach him. She lost her hands in the long, deep gash, but he had already bled out. Jack pulled Jill away.

"God, Jill, this was supposed to be for show," he shouted as he frantically tried to keep hold of her fighting armored body.

She roared again, but retreated. They both fell back to their trailers of armies, leaving Marcos and Audra with Satomi. Audra reached for Satomi, who sobbed over the dead man. Satomi wrenched away.

"What have you done?" Satomi yelled out.

"We have to go," said Audra calmly, even though her body was shaking and all she could hear was blood throbbing in her ears.

"You can't take me," Satomi said resignedly, still clutching the man. "Their army."

"No army," said Audra without explanation. "Do they have a way to make more? Where do they make those *things*?"

"My lab's over there, but we aren't infecting people. I don't understand. I thought you had a deal... " She had sat up, but still whimpered.

"I do. Just not with who you think. This whole place is coming down."

She gave Marcos a nod and he ran over to the trailer Satomi had pointed to. Looking inside, he gave another nod confirming its contents. He unstopped and lit a couple Molotovs before throwing them in.

"Noo," cried out Satomi, rushing forward. Audra grabbed her. Satomi was slick with blood and tears. Her arms flailed as she tried to gain traction and reach the trailer.

"Greenly's scientists won't have anything," explained Audra.

"Greenly?" Another large explosion at the front of the

convoy sounded. Satomi's body went still. "You went to Greenly?"

"I told them there was an army on the road. I figured they wouldn't care for the threat. I'm taking care of things, like I promised. Now come with me. We have to go."

"To hell I'm coming with you! God, I have to go save Peter."

Satomi ripped herself away from Audra. Audra couldn't grab hold again of her slim limbs. Satomi took off down the road, heading toward Greenly's people. Audra gave one last look at the laboratory to make sure it was burning, then chased after her rescue. She had never imagined Satomi would be so uncooperative. Who was Peter? She had no option but to follow the dark-haired woman, who was making distance, fast.

Audra passed burning vans, the work of Greenly's men after they decided they had no use for them. She was glad Marcos had burned the laboratory. They would have spared that one. Audra turned to look behind her to see Marcos trying to keep up. Audra looked down to see familiar dark curly hair and the young man zombied and dead on the ground.

Dennis.

Satomi didn't notice. She sprinted until she skidded to a stop in front of a strange stoop attached to a trailer.

"Don't hurt him!" she warned as she knocked on the door. "He's innocent."

'Innocent' was a funny word. Was Dennis innocent? She didn't know.

There was muffled shuffling heard inside. Audra put her hand on her dagger despite Satomi's warning. Slowly the door opened and an older man poked his head out.

"Time for tea?" he asked.

"No, Peter. I need you to come with me," said Satomi,

holding out her hand.

Peter looked around. The commotion was farther up the road but here it was quiet. He seemed to be left on his own.

"Peter, please?" she asked again.

He looked confused, but he put his hand in hers.

"Where are we going?"

"We're going into the woods to gather dandelion for the tea," Satomi offered.

His face perked up at her suggestion. *Who the hell?*

Audra shook her head and muttered, "We can't take him. Too slow."

Satomi wheeled around, his hand still in hers. "You might be bent on destruction, but I'm not. Do what you need to do. I'll take Peter home myself."

Audra glared at the person she had done all this for. Satomi seemed to have no appreciation for their current condition. The place was burning down around them.

"Get away from him!" someone shouted behind them. Damn.

Jack. Peter let go of Satomi's hand and scrambled down the stoop, pushing both women out of the way.

"Thank God you're OK," said Jack, crying.

"Where's your sister?" asked Peter, comforting the younger man.

"I'm, I'm not sure. We got separated. There was an explosion..." Jack shook. They didn't let go of each other.

Maybe Satomi would be OK to leave this Peter with Jack. "Look we need to go," encouraged Audra.

The squealing of tires and a merciless laugh filled the air as a jeep came barreling down the road. They were too late. Audra and Jack steered Satomi and Peter off the road and toward the woods. Jack and Marcos started to follow, but noticed Audra wasn't leaving. Audra couldn't stand to let Greenly see her run.

She was surprised Greenly had left the safety of her fences.

"Audra. Pleasure seeing you here." Her eyes gleamed.

She stood up on the platform on the back of the jeep, one of her feet raised on something. Her guards stood near her. Two more men came around the jeep and lowered the tailgate.

There lay a body with a blond braid, Greenly's foot firmly on her head.

Jack cried out before falling to his knees. "No, no, no..." he pleaded.

"Glad we could work together," Greenly continued.

Jack was not too stricken to hear the words. He looked to Audra. "You brought this on us?"

Audra blinked. She had brought all of this down on all of them. How else would she keep her family alive? Smoke and the smell of fuel wrapped around the highway.

"Don't worry," comforted Greenly. "She's not working with you, or me. This girl murdered her own sister to get out of some debts. She's out just for herself."

She turned to Audra with a new nastiness. "I know you're destroying what we're trying to create."

"A world under your thumb?" she retorted. She glanced behind her to see if anyone was approaching from behind. Fighting could be heard off in the distance.

Greenly and her crow's feet smiled. "A stable world. Where no one is hungry. Where no one is threatened by others, sick or otherwise."

"They aren't threats. They're people. We work together, eat together, and fight together. We don't hide behind our corporate walls and milk the people."

"Sure, you just kill them instead," she referenced her lost corral. "I'm afraid you won't be doing much of anything anymore, either. You're wanted for breach of contract and crimes against Lysent. You'll be tried and punished," said Greenly.

They should have been long gone. Greenly's men encompassed them. Audra noticed Manny and Blue in the group. Manny winked at her. He licked his lips and left spittle on his mustache.

"Let them go," said Jack. "I own this army and I'll give them to you in return for us here."

"I'm sorry. I believe your army is already mine. I took out your sister. I can take out others," said Greenly dismissively.

Tears streamed down Jack's face.

"I'll tell my men to stand down. You'll lose no one else. Please just let me take them." His voice cracked.

"An army for you five?" Greenly nodded her casual agreement.

Jack immediately stuck his fingers into his mouth and gave a shrill whistle. The commotion died down as the men surrendered.

"Leave," she commanded.

Jack, Marcos, and Audra walked into the woods to meet Satomi and Peter. Audra kept her hand on her dagger. Had Jack sacrificed his entire community just to kill Audra with his bare hands? It didn't matter much. It was important to leave before Greenly realized how nearly worthless her spoils were.

"I'm not going to hurt you," he said before they got within earshot of the others.

"Why not?"

Tears streamed, kept streaming. He had lost his sister. The place he had called home.

"I'm not like that. We were never like that," he said simply. Audra was surprised that her heart believed him.

CHAPTER SEVENTEEN
OUTBREAK

The sun hung high in the cloudless sky, but the tall pine trees provided cover. Spots of scattered light fell on the ground as they made their trek to Osprey Point. Audra's concern about Peter's speed was unfounded. Both Jack and Peter were strong hikers. They marched along without complaint.

"You didn't have to surrender for us," ventured Audra as she rounded her way around a rock outcropping. She'd have found a way out. It did seem like a peace offering, but Audra wondered why he wasn't more dedicated to his uninfected men.

"We had already lost. Whoever that lady was - she had our army. I just wanted to walk away with my dad. I'm sorry we ever picked this fight."

"That lady's Greenly and she doesn't have your army,"

shared Audra. "We cured them."

Jack didn't look to her. Instead he laughed and shook his head.

"What?" asked Audra.

"When we figured out the cure wasn't permanent, we decided to go a different route. That's how the soldier serum and the byproducts came about."

"Dr. Bren-?" said Peter, stopping. Satomi gently nudged him along. He didn't finish his question. Jack helped his father navigate the rocky terrain.

Jack continued, "The cure especially doesn't work on the soldiers. They'll be back to themselves in two days tops. That Greenly will figure it out. You handed her an army."

"The notes were true?" asked Satomi, looking to Jack as she put a supporting hand on Peter's shoulder to help him keep his balance.

"What notes?" asked Audra.

"Dr. Bren's notes," she said as if that explained things. "At first I thought your soldier serum was a detour in your attempts to cure people, but I realized you already had a cure."

"That's right. We had an antidote to the z-virus immediately. Things weren't too bad, but when people eventually reverted, all hell broke loose. That's when Dr. Bren created the soldiers to protect us."

"But their cure is different," stated Audra, attempting to understand.

"Formula-wise, they're the same," said Satomi. "Lysent stockpiles."

Jack helped his father over a large fallen log. "That thing we asked for - Satomi said she could help our father with it. I'm sorry we put on such a show. Jill's idea, but I followed along. It seemed the safest. I didn't think..."

Audra thought on Satomi's pleas to work with Jack and Jill. She thought of a family, not unlike her own, that did whatever they could to survive and protect themselves. Had she built up her real enemy at this family's expense?

*   *   *

They heard the shouts before they had even reached the fences of Osprey Point. Fear flashed in Audra's heart. She took off in a sprint down the gravelly road.

"What is happening here?!" Audra shouted as she waved to them to open the gates and to allow the others behind her to come in as well.

"An outbreak!" shouted the woman above.

An outbreak? How?

"Where is he? In the lab?"

"You mean 'they'. They're in the mess hall," the guard shouted at her back. Audra stopped to turn to see if she was serious. Her stomach sank. How did it get into the mess hall? That didn't make any sense.

"Is Dwyn back?" she shouted up to them.

"No, you're the first ones back."

Her heart sank. Dwyn and the others should have been back by now. She felt a sudden urge to run out and find them. Her crew appeared through the gate, breathless with their run. It brought her back to reality. She needed to deal with this, here.

"Satomi, clear the lab lobby now," she ordered. Satomi nodded.

Audra hesitantly pulled out her dagger for what seemed the hundredth time today. She couldn't help but look at the sun reaching its last arc - it was dinner time. The mess hall would be full. Jack came up beside her, his armor now looking much more appropriate. They stood on either side of the door.

"You don't have to," said Audra.

"I know."

With a nod, Audra opened the door wide enough to see inside. No one ran out. Were they all already...?

"Help!" someone called out. No. Some person was still in there.

Audra slipped through the door and entered with her back against the wall. Jack came up beside her and closed the door securely behind them. The tables and chairs had been turned and toppled over. Remnants of food joined blood splatter on the floor and walls. This couldn't be happening. Not here. Not now. Audra fought the urge to close her eyes and wish for a different world. She got a nudge from Jack. She took a deep breath.

Three, no, four zoms. Zoms. That's what they were. They weren't her friends, her new community. They were a threat. Two people cowered in the corner fending off one of the zoms with a chair. A second zom careened toward them. Another pair clawed at the kitchen door.

"I'll take the four." She motioned to the kitchen door. "That leads to the kitchen. I bet everyone is in there. Come out with me then slip back in. Subdue or kill any threat in there."

"I'll try to capture them."

"Thank you," Audra whispered, steeling herself to be bait and to encourage a chase.

"HEY Zs! Here Zs!" she yelled out, clapping her hands. The zom reaching for the two men behind the chair paid her no mind. This emboldened her. She picked up a leg of a broken white pine chair, jumped over a long thin table, and jabbed it into the zom's ribs. Blond hair whipped around. The face looked ragged with emotion and hunger.

Lisa.

Shit. Audra had stumbled upon her the day they cured Gordon. She was one of their first outside cures and she still reminded her of her sister. Audra took care not to slip on the red sauce or blood. She ignored the two's fearful faces as she drew Lisa toward her.

She shifted and found the wall opposite her exit, two clambering for her now. They tripped over chairs and dived after smacking into a table. She followed the wall until she reached the kitchen door with two zoms beating and scratching at the space where their prey had disappeared. How had they transitioned so quickly?

She swung and hit shoulders. They turned their heads at crooked angles in twin-like unison, veins spread from their cold eyes. Grayness tinged their skin except for the bright red spots on a forearm and a shoulder - a declaration of what had taken them over. Audra sighed relief at the sight of their clean mouths. Maybe this would be it.

Yells from the kitchen.

"Hush!" Audra called out. "I'm trying to lead them away!"

"It's Audra," she heard in hushed voices. "Oh thank heavens, it's Audra. It's going to be OK..."

Audra pulled away to let the twins join her other two. She now had her small herd.

"That's impressive," said Jack from the door.

"Clear out the plaza," she instructed him. It was a dumb and dangerous idea to lead a herd into the open air of their community, but she didn't want her community to think that if they got bit again, she'd just sink a dagger into their brains. They were over that, weren't they?

The command was unnecessary. The plaza was already empty. She appreciated everyone tucked away with their doors shut. This could be the end of the outbreak here. Jack waited on the wayside to reenter. The guards watched from above, no longer looking to the outside but to the creeping threat inside, the safety of the complex imploding. Audra saw the door to the lab lobby stood open. And she began to head that way.

Maybe their transition wasn't complete, but still the zoms' open mouths seemed unnaturally long, as if they could unhinge and swallow her whole. Saliva fell from their chins. Behind them, Jack slipped back into the mess hall to help those previously trapped in the kitchen.

"Oh my god!" cried someone from Audra's left. Shit. "Is that-?"

"Back inside and be quiet!" Audra shouted as her zoms found new trajectories.

The person scrambled to get back inside, but someone held the door shut on him, apparently having seen what lay outside.

"Holy hell! Let me in!" he cried. The door slammed open and shut in its frame, causing a racket. Audra raced to the four. They were no longer interested in her, no matter how loudly she yelled. She threw her baton at one of their heads; it did nothing but push them forward.

"Run to another door!" Audra called out. He turned at the command. Seeing the four scrambling toward him, he braced himself against the door and yelled out. His mouth and eyes were wide with fear.

"GO NOW!" barked Audra as she sprinted to get between them. The boy finally came to his senses and ran off toward another building. Feet kicking high. Audra scooted right behind him to create a visually large moving mass. Someone opened the door in the next building to receive them. He jumped onto the concrete stoop and raced inside.

"Not me," called out Audra as the boy's heels disappeared into the building.

Audra confirmed the door closed with a dry click before she trotted past it. Now they were back on her. Audra pulled away from the buildings and did a wide circle back to the lobby. The mess hall's door was closed, but people watched from the windows. Jack had pulled them out of the kitchen.

Audra ran straight through the front lobby of the lab, not stopping to admire the outdated panel wood walls. Satomi shut the door behind her as she scooted into the laboratory's main area. Audra sprinted through and out the back door to round the building. All four were in the lobby, scraping on the interior door.

Audra closed the exterior door and slid down against it. Her hand arrived at her brow to wipe the stinging salt from her eyes, but she found it covered in someone's blood. Down her arm was just as messy. She didn't get to clean up or rest. Satomi came around and gave her a hand up. She had tears in her eyes, but that wasn't surprising. She watched Satomi leave for the medical office to go see Ryder. For Audra, it was time to find out about the kitchen. Was anyone else bitten?

*　　*　　*

"Satomi, clear the lab lobby now!" Audra yelled to her as she and Jack ran off to the mess hall. Marcos climbed up to speak with the guards. Peter stood with her, dumbfounded. She felt the same.

Infected in the mess hall? The thought filled her with fear. She had done so much to take precautions. What had happened here?

Satomi nodded but she wasn't sure that Audra saw.

They used to keep infected in the lobby before they established the medical office. The medical office - Satomi's mind flashed to Ryder, who would be in there, just a building away. She yearned to see her, just a glimpse of her form to make sure she was all right - that she was real. Both her time at Osprey Point and at Jack's and Jill's convoy seemed to blur. Which was her life? Satomi shook her head clear. There were higher priority tasks right now. And Peter was one of them.

She ushered Peter through the plaza. He stopped at the fountain.

"Why isn't it on?"

"Um, we turned it off in preparation for winter," she said to give him a simple answer.

He looked up to the sky as if he expected snow to fall. She nudged him along and he mumbled as he followed. They walked past the medical office and Satomi tried to steal a glance through the window, but they had been covered for privacy. Her idea.

Behind the medical office was a converted office for sleeping quarters. She opened the door and found no one in the front area. Here, Peter could be safe while she helped the others.

"Peter, please, I need you to go in here for just a moment."

Peter seemed to finally notice the doorway. He stopped in his tracks and stared in horror.

"I don't want to go in there," Peter refused. "I want to go home."

"Just for a moment," she pleaded. She needed to clear the lab lobby.

"You can't make me! I'M NOT A PRISONER!" he shouted. His eyes flew open.

"You're right. You're not a prisoner. This is Osprey

Point. It's your new home but I need you to stay here until I come and get you. Is that OK?"

"It's not OK!" he shouted. He seemed really disturbed. He moved to step away. Satomi wasn't sure what to do. Burning car tires uselessly came to mind.

"I'm a prisoner!" he yelled.

"Why do you think that?" she asked in a quiet voice, hoping to reason with him.

"Because I did awful things," he replied, his voice lowering to match hers. Satomi went to put her hand on his arm. He pulled away and shrank into himself.

"No, you didn't. You're a good man, Peter," she cajoled.

"No, I'm not. I experimented!" He looked wildly around, not finding comfort from his strange environment.

"Experimented?" Was he gleaning new vocabulary and delusions from Satomi's chatter? She'd have to watch what she said around him from now on. She had frightened him. He started crying.

"You're going to experiment on me!"

"I'm not." She lied, a little. His treatment would be experimental, but she wasn't doing that right now. Right now, she just needed him safe.

"You're going to experiment on me like I did on the others."

"...the others?" she hesitated.

"Super Soldiers! We were going to make people better. It had to be done, right? The virus didn't have to be bad." Peter shook his head. His white hair danced on his head.

Satomi had never heard Peter say anything about the virus before. What did he know?

"I was going to be a hero. Make people better."

"How?" Satomi dared to ask. The hairs on her arms

prickled.

"My serums! I made soldiers. My next round of experiments didn't go well... made me sick."

Satomi froze. This wasn't early-onset dementia or Alzheimer's disease? This was... self-inflicted? She tried her old test, but this time added another trigger.

"I'm Dr. Satomi Asai. Pleasure to meet you, Doctor...?"

He shook his head to clear it.

"Dr. Peter Bren," he said as he offered his hand.

That woman in the car wasn't Dr. Bren. He was.

She had risked her friends' lives to save the originator of the soldier serum.

And now, he was stopping her from helping. Tears slipped down her cheeks and the top of her head burned. Satomi pushed him into the building a little rougher than she intended. He fell to the ground. He glared at her betrayal. It didn't matter; she had friends to help. She slammed the door before he could get up.

"I'm sorry!" she said. She wasn't sure who that was directed towards, but she was.

*　　*　　*

Audra knocked on the mess hall door. It opened without ceremony with Jack just inside the entrance.

"Good running," he told her. Audra nodded and looked around. Twelve people inside. Some sat shaking on chairs, some busied themselves by cleaning up, others helped those who might be in shock.

"Are they OK?" asked a girl.

The zoms were still family.

Audra smiled a small smile. "They're fine. They're in the lobby of the laboratory. The scientists will prepare antidotes immediately. But first, I need to know what happened here."

"It was my girlfriend, Lisa," said a woman being comforted on a chair. Her shaking slowed as she spoke.

"When did she get bit?" asked Audra, kneeling down beside her. Although she imagined that her battle-torn look was not comforting.

"She... didn't."

The woman supporting her tapped her on the shoulder. "You don't get to say that. Now she got bit somewhere. Did you guys go out? Maybe to get some privacy?"

"No. That's what I'm telling you. We've been inside the fences. We've been together. Like hip to hip for the last three days. She wasn't bit."

"Then what happened?" Audra asked gently.

"She was just sick. Had a cold or something. I thought it was the season change. I offered to bring her food from the mess hall, but she said it'd help to move around." She pulled her arms around herself as if she was cold.

"What were her symptoms?"

"Fever. Chills. I'm sorry, I know she shouldn't have gone into the mess hall. She could have given everyone the flu."

"It wasn't the flu," corrected the woman at her shoulder.

"I know that now," she said flatly.

"It's OK. We'll get to the bottom of it. She was bit somewhere, somehow," encouraged Audra.

"Maybe she sneaked off," the standing woman offered.

That made the girl whimper and start shaking again.

The door swung open and Peter raced inside. His face opened with terror as he searched the faces in the room. He found the one he knew. Jack's.

"It's OK, Dad. It's OK," Jack comforted him.

Peter buried his face in his son's chest and cried. Jack held him fiercely. Audra felt a weird twinge for this broken family. They still had someone flesh and blood to hug and to hold. Audra would give anything for that. To belong. She understood why they had gone to such great lengths to stay together. Wouldn't she - hadn't she - done the same?

As the people in the mess hall quietly dispersed, a head of brown curls peeked through the doorway.

Dwyn.

She ran into his arms. They radiated warmth and safety through her body. She deposited her face into his neck and musk.

"What took you so long?" she murmured.

Maybe she did have a family. He felt like home.

"I... I had to carry Ziv's body back."

Ziv's body?

Audra pulled back and saw the tears filling Dwyn's perfect green eyes. He rubbed the back of his neck with his hand, staring down at his feet.

"I sent him in there..." said Audra. She felt her tears come on too.

Dwyn met her eyes. "No. He volunteered. Developed the mass cure and died making sure his plan succeeded."

The mass cure - which Jack said wouldn't even work. Jack. Jack's crew had done this. She turned in Dwyn's arms to reconcile what she knew about Jack. He had driven a half zom army, kidnapped Satomi. He had also stopped his sister, loved his father, and helped her twice today.

"I'm sorry about Ziv," said Jack. "I understand if you need me to leave, but I'd like to trade for some of Satomi's expertise if she's willing."

"I can't think about that now," said Audra in a short tone. "We have an incident to investigate and zoms to treat." She dismissed it for now.

"Investigate? What is there to investigate?" asked Dwyn.

"I don't know how she got infected. We need to find her bite and figure out what happened."

"She was infected before, right?" asked Jack.

"Yes, but that was a long time ago. We cured her."

"You cured her for a while, yes. She probably reverted."

Audra remembered what Jack and Satomi had discussed in the woods. Was it true?

"The cure... it doesn't work all the time," repeated Jack. "We thought it did at first, but it got slowly bad. People we've cured have gotten sick again. We haven't been able to permanently cure a soldier ever. Dr. Bren told us the virus either mutated or the cure was never perfect to begin with."

"We'll see. She probably wandered off," Audra borrowed from the unhelpful friend. "She'll have a bite."

CHAPTER EIGHTEEN
PATIENT ZERO

With the infected safely secured inside the front lobby and Audra safe, Satomi made a beeline to the medical office to see Ryder. She'd better be still in the medical ward. No way should she be discharged already. It had only been a week - or more? Satomi couldn't recall.

She needed to hug her friend and cry on her shoulder. Her failure was sinking in. She hadn't saved a family torn apart by illness. They had created it. She had tried to do no harm, but she had. The universe was much more complicated than she had given credit. Now she just needed something she knew was solid.

She opened the door to the office and could already hear odd sounds. Was Ryder in pain? She sprinted into the doorway, before staggering back. The soldier Satomi had treated with leg splints had been moved from the laboratory. But no one was here to watch him.

He had been restrained, but one hand was bloodied, broken, and free. His shoulder contorted with dislocation as he had pulled himself off the bed. He had torn down the partition and reached toward the next bed, where a figure shaped like Ryder was snoozing under the covers. Her back turned.

Satomi saw red. This *thing* was after her love. He would get to her and soon. Satomi raced to the counter across from the beds and ripped open a drawer to find her tool. A yell escaped her lips as she drove her scalpel into his craniocervical junction. He had no idea she was in the room before he was gone. His body crumpled.

Both of them slumped on the ground. Satomi's chest heaved high and low. She couldn't get air. The panic of everything hit her. Her home - Osprey Point - had been attacked. She had been kidnapped and forced to work for her captors. She'd slept in a crappy car and feared for her life. Her best friend had been inches from death.

She looked ahead at her medical supplies. They grounded her, reminded her that she was on the verge of hyperventilating. She slowed her breathing and tried to gain control.

First, do no harm.

She had broken her promise. She looked over to Ryder, who still slept. They must still be giving her narcotics. As she gazed on her friend, a sudden calmness overtook her. She was worth a promise broken. Satomi let the scalpel clatter to the ground beside her. Maybe the oath only applied to the world before. She went to her friend and gently hugged her awake.

She'd settle for doing what was right.

* * *

"I know this isn't the best time, but... this is important," Satomi heard Audra say as Satomi entered the back way into the lab. The stark white walls, small windows, and messy counters filled her sights and her heart. Oh, how she missed this place. Sure, the equipment was ancient, rusting, and cracked, but at least the building wasn't on wheels.

"Funny," Satomi interrupted. "I was going to say the same thing."

The occupants of the lab, Audra, Dwyn, and Gordon turned to look at her. They were dirty with battle and the blood of their enemies. So was Satomi.

"Oh my God. Is that blood?" Audra rushed over. She pulled Satomi onto a stool and began examining the doctor for wounds.

Satomi shivered. Gordon brought her a heavy blanket as she explained what had happened. He leaned up against the counter near her. Dwyn sat on the counter, kicking and dangling his feet, without much concern for the fragility of the equipment around him.

"Are you sure he's dead?" asked Audra. Yes, she was sure.

"Why was he moved anyway?" Satomi asked.

"Uh, because Ziv had cured him," said Gordon with a numbed tone.

A heavy silence filled the room at the mention of Ziv's name.

"So, all the soldiers?" Dwyn asked. He had stopped kicking.

Audra did not address Dwyn, but instead she turned to Satomi. "I need you to check our patient zero. We need to find out how she got sick again."

Satomi remembered Dr. Bren's notes. She nodded slowly, letting the scratchy blanket fall to the floor.

"What do you mean?" asked Gordon.

Audra stumbled, "Just check the body. Find the bite," she directed him.

Gordon nodded and cleared an area to receive their subject.

"Which one is patient zero?" asked Satomi.

"Lisa."

Dwyn left to dispose of the body in the medical ward. In just a few minutes, Audra and Gordon had bound Lisa and eased her onto the cleared laminate counter. Lisa writhed, arching and twisting her torso, and Satomi struggled to examine her. Her hands still shook with the adrenaline of before, but felt warmer with a medical duty to perform.

"We don't waste anesthetic on the dead," she whispered before she realized she was speaking. No one asked her what she meant, thankfully.

Satomi's gloved hands and observant eyes looked over all the likely spots, then the less likely spots, then the entirety of the body. Lisa's body was perfect; none of her skin was broken. A scar prickled at her ankle, a bodily reminder of her first bite, but otherwise Lisa's skin was flawless.

"There is no bite," Satomi reported.

"Maybe it healed?" asked Audra hopefully.

"Her first bite has healed. But I don't see anything else."

"What does that mean?" asked Gordon.

"Possibly she came in contact with infectious bodily fluids, blood, saliva, sexual fluids," said Satomi, not wanting to jump to conclusions, just because she had seen it written in a mad doctor's books.

"Or?" pushed Audra.

Lisa was just one case, Satomi told herself. And the soldier with the broken legs was given the antiviral via an experimental delivery system. He couldn't be counted.

"When was she cured?" Satomi asked.

"Near our start," replied Audra, looking down at the woman's large, foggy eyes and tangled hair.

Satomi looked down and saw the same. Of course, Lisa. Satomi wondered why she hadn't recognized her. Their faces seemed to distort in their sickness.

"It's possible," Satomi confessed. "I would think it would have happened a lot sooner, though. The virus could live in small dormant quantities. If something upended the chemistry of the brain or the virus found a way to adapt, then it could take back over." Dr. Bren had studied it for years and hadn't figured it out in his part of the country. Would she be able to figure it out?

Satomi continued, "I can test her viral load for any abnormalities. If it's mutated, we won't know if it's because she was exposed to a mutated virus or if it mutated within her – "

"Not now. It can wait," Audra interrupted. "We all need rest. You, especially."

Satomi didn't continue her ramble and didn't argue. She could barely keep upright over Lisa. Her body was shutting down. She watched Gordon and Audra move Lisa back to the lobby. Then Gordon escorted Satomi to her bed. Her real bed.

*　　*　　*

"Do you really think the cure isn't working?" asked Gordon quietly as he helped Audra return Lisa to the front room.

"I don't know," Audra replied, knowing she was

speaking to someone who had been cured. Almost everyone here had been. Were they all at risk for reverting to their mindless, violent, shuffling selves? No, it couldn't be. The cure was permanent.

It had to be.

Otherwise, what were they fighting for? Audra couldn't imagine this hell without hope.

"You'll remain healthy for your girl. Don't worry," assured Audra.

CHAPTER NINETEEN
MEMORIAL

It wasn't long before Gordon and Satomi had news for Audra. After interviews, an investigation, and further testing, it was concluded that Lisa was only infected now because she had been previously infected. She had reverted somehow. Their first case of the antidote failing.

Audra stared at an empty beaker on the drying rack by the sink, as if it would give her the answers she needed.

"We need to let Greenly know," said Audra to no one really.

"Know what?" asked Gordon.

"About this isolated case. They can look out for their own potential issues. An outbreak in their townships could wipe *us* out."

Yelling in the plaza interrupted them.

The trio, almost forgetting to go the back way, walked

out to see what the commotion was. They had postponed treating the group from the mess hall outbreak, much to the rest of the residents' disapproval.

A man lay on the fountain wall, his chest rising unusually tall. Audra knew him, a runner - a protege for sure. He had probably plowed through the plaza, almost being clipped by the gate. He stood up and wobbled a little with the blood rush.

He still had a lot to learn.

"When they got them... They... They were healthy, but some were not," he started.

"The army?" Audra asked.

He nodded. His hands held his sides - either to keep his rib cage at bay or to tell his lungs that yes, indeed, he was trying to breathe.

He tried again, "Over the next few days, they went back to being brainwashed soldiers. All of them. She has all of them." He gasped and tilted forward on his hips.

Audra took a hand and pulled his chest upright.

"You'll get more air this way if you aren't nauseous," she recommended as she fought her own nausea. Greenly with a half zom army made her stomach churn.

As if corporate power was not enough, Greenly had now been delivered a formidable offense. Audra had all but giftwrapped them. She felt herself turn green. What had she created? What would they face now?

"You wanted to talk to Greenly?" said the skeptical voice of Gordon.

Audra nodded dumbly.

"How are you going to get close with her new army?" he asked.

Good question.

She didn't have an answer for that - or any of it, for that matter.

*   *   *

In all the chaos, Dwyn and Gordon had buried Ziv. Audra had made trips to the river for large, smooth, speckled stones to stack and mark his grave. Their community, still in shock with the news of the reversion and never having enjoyed Ziv's brusque personality, had paid little attention. His heroic feat to save them all had been relegated to a futile effort. Another failure on their list.

Audra became familiar with the experience. The people of Osprey Point had liked the idea of her out in the woods, bringing people in - most people owed their lives to her - but this past week had shown them she was no hero. She had possibly wakened them, just for them to fall back into madness and pain.

They gathered at his grave to pay their respects. Satomi kept her arm around Ryder, who used a crutch to hold herself steady due to her injury or Satomi's tight connection, Audra wasn't sure. Gordon and Dwyn stood nearby. Audra looked down to Ziv. He was where he'd want to be. Right next to Vesna.

"When I first met you all, I didn't understand why Ziv was out here," started Audra. "He didn't seem to want to be out here, and he didn't have any qualms about letting us know."

Some giggles in the tiny audience. Then, a sniffle.

"But the thing about doing the right thing - is that you don't have to do it enthusiastically. You just have to do it. And when forced into situations, Ziv did the right thing.

"Ziv was loyal. He held onto Vesna's ideals and friendship long after she passed. He died making Vesna's plan to aerosolize the antidote finally a reality.

"Though they reverted, it gave us the time we needed to save Satomi. He did that. Sometimes it might feel like all we do is for naught. That's how this world is now. Most of what we do, try to do, see done - is futile. But it's still important to do.

"When Ziv stood here as we watched over and spoke over Vesna's memorial, he said that he wanted to be strong. He wanted to be here for us. And he was. And that says a lot about a person. A promise of change kept.

"He did both *no harm* and *harm* when needed. Rather than doggedly stick to old principles, he assessed and did what was correct. We can only hope to perform such a task as we go on about our days with both these two showing us the way. They've died to make sure that we're OK in the end. And we will be OK in the end, because of them."

Dwyn went to hug her and to hold her. And despite being in sight of everyone in their group, Audra let him. She let him wrap his arms around her, because they felt good. Because if it was all for nothing, then what did it matter? They could only do the good and right things.

"Thank you," he whispered into her hair.

"For what?"

"For sharing what we all needed to hear."

"It's what Ziv told us with his life," she said into his chest.

"But you gave it words."

Audra's tears flowed freely and did not stop for a while.

* * *

The salt dried on her neck and collarbone as Audra returned with the others. She walked past the mess hall again, diverting her eyes, not able to bring herself to enter - those men fending off Lisa with just a chair. It could happen again. When? Weeks from now? Days?

Audra looked back at the gate, which was now shut. But the forest beyond their chain-link fences called to her. Maybe she'd go back out. Lose herself in the fall leaves. Before she could decide, her escape was thwarted.

"Hi Jack."

He and his father were allowed temporary heavily-guarded stay while Audra decided what to do with them.

"It's Peter. Peter Bren, Jr." He offered his hand. Audra lifted her hand to meet it. "I assume Satomi explained who my father is."

"Yes, but why don't *you* tell me?" They sat down on the limestone wall. Audra stretched out her legs, crossing them at the ankle. She propped herself up with her hands.

Jack's - or Peter's - eyes went shiny. "Dad's a scientist. Worked for Lysent in D.C. He knew exactly what was going on when the outbreaks started, stockpiled the antiviral. We had it made, considering. Then, it stopped working, or never did work - I dunno. So Dad decided to modify it. He thought that if he turned the zombies into soldiers, we'd be better protected. He even tried to enhance us. He started with himself - you can see that didn't work out well."

Audra listened, staring at the little grasses cropping up around the cracked concrete. Her own memories were very different from the start, and yet, here they were.

Peter continued, "Dad was the scientist, but I was the builder. I built the moving convoy when Dad got sick. We figured we'd seek out other Lysent scientists. Maybe they could continue Dad's work. I guess we got out of hand. The names. Our stupid plastic thrones. The fighting. We just assumed everyone out here was bad, deserved it, I guess. Jill's idea to burn that zom. Figured they're incurable anyway and it'd scare Satomi." His voice honeyed as he talked about his sister.

"If you knew your army wouldn't really be cured, why'd you surrender?" asked Audra. It was something that had been bothering her.

"We were... unprepared for you. Greenly came too fast. It was over before I knew it. Evelyn was dead. I realized I just wanted my dad - as flawed as he is - as flawed as Evelyn was."

Evelyn *was* flawed. So was Audra. They'd both tried to rely on destruction, and look where it had gotten them. She thought of Satomi's mission statement, those Latin words that directed her path, and she thought of Ziv's reluctant but correct choices. She knew what to do.

"You can stay if you want. We don't have a lot of free space. Our enemy has a virtually unstoppable army. And we're an outbreak waiting to happen... but we can live together. Help each other."

"Thank you. I don't mind tight quarters. I can bunk with my dad."

Audra understood. If she had family left, she wouldn't let them out of her sight either.

"We'll ask Satomi if she'd like to help with your father," she said, standing up and stretching.

They both knew she would.

Audra brushed through the gate. She started with a slow jog to prevent any protesting muscles, and so that Osprey Point didn't think she was fleeing, even if that's how she felt. As soon as she was out of eyesight, she light-stepped into the woods. She preferred it over the road. You had to dodge and juke. You had to be clever with your steps, else get caught up or slip. Her cadence increased and her speed picked up. The lighter wisps of loose hair moved this way and that against her neck with her rhythm. It was a rhythm that made Audra feel in sync with both nature and herself. She felt more her, the farther she ran.

She would not get to run long. The sun danced around the trees at eye level, threatening to go under as Audra flirted with dusk. She looked up to see orange and red cresting the sky. What should have been a pleasant sunset seemed to be an omen of blood to come. It pushed her forward, faster and faster. She careened through the woods, jumping over logs, skidding in leaves, light branches scraping her face and chest. She'd continue. She'd keep going. Just as she was doing now.

Audra would have loved to run as far as she could in one direction, set up camp for the night, and be alone. She would have loved to gaze at the stars and watch the satellites fly by. She'd pretend she could be as distant as those satellites, so far away that she could only see peace. No warring factions, no wandering sick, no desolate cities serving as harsh growing grounds for the weeds. Instead, she'd see green, and blue, so much blue. Audra wondered what the ocean looked like now. She hadn't seen it since she was oh so very young. How blue was it? Had it changed now that man was basically gone? Would man eventually be gone?

Running until night overtook her was not a viable plan at the moment. They needed her to be present in Osprey Point. Audra reluctantly turned back around. She started toward her community, with all its flaws and with all the trouble they were in. She ran towards her home, whether she considered it that or not.

Home would have Belinda. It would have family.

Belinda, it had not. Family, possibly.

CHAPTER TWENTY
LYSENT'S ANNOUNCEMENT

It turned out Audra didn't need to reach out to Lysent. As she and her small core group approached Lysent headquarters, an announcement was already in progress. They hung outside the fences, just within earshot, a place Audra was familiar with. Audra recalled Greenly's previous announcements - the cure, the tagging program, their stance on rebellion as they executed Vesna. Greenly's announcements always changed her life.

And this one wouldn't be any different.

Larange Greenly stood in front of the Lysent plaza. Her mahogany podium shined with polish. Audra tried to decipher what was different. Greenly was sandwiched between two guards, different from ones Audra had seen previously. And the protesters. They used to be a permanent fixture for these announcements and were nowhere to be found. Vesna's execution must have put an end to that.

"I have grave news today," Greenly's voice carried to them. They continued to hide in the brush. "You may be familiar with the group to the southeast of us. They are a small group who stole the antiviral from our trains, antiviral meant to go to one of you. You may have heard that they are curing people without regard to financial status, which I'm sure will hurt them come winter time when they find themselves stretched too thin.

I have done my best to protect you from them. One of their leaders had to be executed on this very stage."

Audra felt the heat rise to her face. Her blood was boiling. How dare Greenly talk about Vesna up there as if any of that was a favor to anyone.

"Unfortunately, their experiments have not ended there. They have stolen other things from us, performed genetic therapies that typically would have been vetted by a review board in times before the infection. Without that oversight, without our oversight, they have done reckless things."

She hesitated, then continued, "At times, I wonder if they weren't doing these irresponsible experiments before the outbreak which led to our troubles today."

"Wow," said Gordon, and he lightly punched Audra in the arm to get her attention. "Did she really just blame us for the zombie plague?"

"I think she did," replied Dwyn, picking some berries from the bush he was behind. "It's smart. If we come out with our proof that Lysent started it, we're pulling papers from OUR laboratory. She'll say, it wasn't Lysent, it was us."

Gordon swore. "Is this what it's all about?"

"I don't think so," said Audra, wishing they would all

hush. Greenly didn't assemble her people just to poke holes in an old story.

"Our scientists have discovered the group out there has experimented too carelessly. They pushed forward with a supposedly 'temperature-stable' antiviral. My scientists avoided this unnecessary upgrade because the proteins show subtle deterioration. Their nonperfect replica seems to be malfunctioning, leaving trace, dormant amounts of the virus in the host. We haven't been able to measure it in any blood test; however, for reasons unknown for now, the viral load can increase and take the host back over."

Greenly knew.

Murmurs and cries filled the plaza.

"I want to be clear!" shouted Greenly over the din. The trained crowd quieted.

"I want to be clear. Anyone cured through Lysent proper is not in danger. The antiviral works, just not the bastardizations found via the black market. The group to our southeast is an outbreak waiting to happen. Their entire community is a ticking time bomb. If you live with anyone cured by one of these underground means, know that you are living alongside a zombie in sleeping.

That's the danger of doing this on your own. That's the danger of no oversight. That's the danger of awakening people without due process!"

"She's blaming us for the whole damn thing," said Dwyn. His berries fell from his hand, forgotten.

"That she is," Audra muttered. She backed even farther from the fence. Suddenly, she didn't want to be seen.

"Holy crap. Do you think she's right?" Gordon asked.

Audra wasn't sure how to answer that.

"She could be lying," she said thoughtfully. "Ja- Peter

said they had the same problem."

"Isn't that a dangerous lie to tell your community?"

"Do you think she cares?" countered Audra. "She just has to keep up the charade until she sows enough discord."

"Enough discord to do what?" asked Dwyn.

"Prime her people for war. To look the other way or cheer when she wipes us out," Audra explained.

"So we're the villains," concluded Gordon. "If I'm the villain... I can't go greet my daughter. I can't approach my family."

It seemed to be sinking in for Gordon. Audra had wondered when it would.

"What do you mean?" asked Dwyn.

"I'm a zombie, in waiting. There's no reason to tell my family I'm here and safe... because I'm not."

Audra's heart crumbled to pieces and her stomach felt pitted. She had been trying to help everyone. Was Lysent right? Was their antiviral flawed? Had they rushed something that shouldn't have been rushed?

"But maybe you can tell them?" asked Dwyn. "Maybe they'd want to know even if... you know, you're still sick."

"I can't! Don't you see! I could turn and destroy everything and everyone near me. I'm a - what did she call me? - a ticking time bomb. I can't be anywhere near my daughter. Ever. For the rest of whatever life I have left."

The others fell silent. It didn't really matter what else Greenly had to say. They had come to warn her, but now there was nothing to do here. Greenly had beat them to the punch. And she had punched hard. It was time to go and mop things up at Osprey Point. And prepare. Prepare for war.

*　*　*

Her legs couldn't carry her back from Lysent fast enough. Audra was ready to get back. Running was now just for transportation - nothing could be achieved by it. No longer would she be out searching for zombies to cure. That was on hold indefinitely. They could be on the verge of a massive outbreak, a wave across the country where survivors and zombies were pitted against each other once more. Were they ready this time? With no cure in sight, how should they treat the sick?

More leaves softened her path than shaded her from the sun. Lysent was correct on another point. Winter was coming. And they needed to be ready. With the crunch of leaves, Dwyn finally asked the question Audra dreaded.

"Do you think it's true?"

"Do I think *what* is true?" she asked to buy time. Was it true that she had lost or would lose everyone she cared about? Was it true that all of what Audra had lived for was worthless, dying, or dead?

"Do you think that those cured by Lysent are OK?"

That wasn't what he was asking. He was asking if *he* was OK. Was he on borrowed time? Would he turn on his family?

Audra had no answer for him.

ABOUT THE AUTHOR

R.M. Hamrick lives in Savannah, Georgia where moss hangs from the oak trees and the humidity can be sliced with a butter knife. She writes the zombie-filled Chasing series and the wacky space opera, Atalan Adventures. She's partnered with a tantrum-throwing Redfoot tortoise and loves board games, craft beer, and odd numbers. Follow her on Patreon.com/rmhamrick